SUSAN A. JENNINGS

When Love Ends Romance Begins

The Narrowboat Romance Series Book 1

[handwritten inscription and signature]

SaRaKa InPrint

First edition

ISBN: 978-0-9959465-6-9

This book was professionally typeset on Reedsy.
Find out more at reedsy.com

In memory of my beloved father
Jack Jennings
1915 - 1986
Captain of our family cabin cruiser Jessica
Remembering so many wonderful days of fun, cruising
Britain's Inland Waterways with you and Mum.

Love and Friendship

Love is like the wild rose-briar,
Friendship like the holly-tree—
The holly is dark when the rose-briar
blooms
But which will bloom most con-
stantly?

The wild rose-briar is sweet in spring,
Its summer blossoms scent the air;
Yet wait till winter comes again
And who will call the wild-briar fair?

Then scorn the silly rose-wreath now
And deck thee with the holly's sheen,
That when December blights thy
brow
He still may leave thy garland green.

EMILY BRONTE

Contents

Foreword

Narrowboats Explained...

When Love Ends, Romance Begins is a romance novel set in, on and around narrowboats and the British inland waterways; a unique and romantic setting but not a familiar one to most readers which is why, below, you will find a brief history of narrowboats and waterways.

My connection to the British inland waterways is strong and memorable. Jack Jennings, my father, owned and operated a boat during my pre-teen and teenage years; a cabin cruiser called *Jessica*. We even lived on the boat for a time. My mother, Betty Jennings, set the boat up as a fully functioning home, a temporary solution when we were between houses.

Jessica, like similar cabin cruisers, and later narrowboats are the equivalent to the North American summer cottage—on the water rather than by the water. The sole purpose: fun and relaxation with family and friends for weekend get-a-ways, relaxing holidays and escaping the city.

We traveled many nautical miles along the inland waterways of Britain's rivers and canals, including a couple of out-to-sea excursions, much to my mother's chagrin. Losing sight of land caused a slight green hue to her cheeks. My father and I enjoyed the excitement of the ocean even if only a few miles offshore. As with many niche activities, a camaraderie and culture develops within the boaters group. My fond memories of those years, boating with my parents, gave me a thorough understanding of the culture.

Styles change over time but the tranquility, peacefulness and sense of comradeship found on the water has not changed. Our boat, *Jessica*, travelled the rivers and some of the canals that allowed for the wider beam boats. In the fifties and sixties, the cabin cruiser was the boat of choice—narrowboats were considered commercial with only a few innovative boaters seeing their potential.

The use of narrowboats started during the British Industrial Revolution, which forced the need for the efficient, economical transportation of bulk commodities between factories and cities. A horse drawn cart on a mud road could not do the job. The first industry to adopt narrowboat transportation, the Staffordshire potteries, prompted a network of narrow canals and locks that grew throughout the country. The wooden narrowboats - not an inch more than 7ft wide and 72ft long and drawn by horses - transported coal, timber, machinery and factory supplies in their large holds. A small cabin at the stern, served as crew quarters for weeks, even months, at a time. These painstakingly slow journeys moved at a steady walk; the crewman alongside the horse on the parallel towpath as it pulled the heavy narrowboat through the canal. As economic times became tougher, instead of hiring crews to handle the narrowboats, whole families lived in the tiny cabin and crewed the boat.

The use of steam engines, and later diesel, replaced horse-power and made the journeys shorter but engines also facilitated the advent of commercial railways. An even more efficient method of transportation, it caused the canal's usefulness to decline and the waterways to fall into disrepair, resulting in the abandonment of commercial narrowboats.

A group of enterprising people recognized the opportunity to convert these commercial narrowboats into floating holiday homes and built cabins where cargo once travelled. The style of the bright, decorative and tiny rear crew cabin was maintained. The insides were fitted with sitting and sleeping areas, mini kitchens and bathrooms—four to five hundred square feet of living space.

The modern luxury narrowboat, a home away from home, is now equipped with modern conveniences: stoves, fridges, TVs, and Wi-Fi. The old-fashioned traditionalists still prefer the wooden converted style but demand for these boats has caused a boom in business for new aluminum purpose-built narrowboats. The tradition of bright colours, motifs and flowers painted on the cabins has flourished together with interesting names, like Dog Days, Lazy Ways and Catch-You-Later.

Marinas expanded to accommodate narrowboats and their owners, some developing into resort style establishments with petrol/gas and maintenance services, pubs, restaurants, hotels, shops and activities. Many pubs along the canals expanded their gardens and built docks and moorings for boat enthusiasts to enjoy a pint and a pub meal.

Willington in South Derbyshire, close to Barrow-on-Trent (where I grew up and where my mother still lives), is one such luxury marina. Mercia Marina gave me the inspiration to write this series of contemporary romance novels.

Bob's Marina, the fictitious marina in *When Love Ends, Romance Begins* is a pared down version of the Mercia Marina with a café and gift store and is closer to what I experienced when boating with my parents. Unlike Mercia Marina, and for the convenience of the story, Bob's Marina has a typical English village at the top of Marina Lane. If you are familiar with the area, you may just recognize some of the descriptions in the books and that's okay.

When Love Ends Romance Begins

A novel of heartbreak, hope and a second chance at love!

Quotes from Thomas Moore

Romantic love is an illusion. Most of us discover this truth at the end of a love affair or else when the sweet emotions of love lead us into marriage and then turn down their flames...

...And soon, too soon, we part with pain, To sail o'er silent seas again.

One

Divorced

∼◦⧼⧽◦∼

"**D**ivorced!"

Katie Saunders stared at the official letter announcing that she and John were no longer married. Why couldn't he have just died? Smashed that ridiculous mid-life crisis sports car or contracted some terrible disease—a long, lingering, debilitating disease? John deserved both.

She wondered, exactly, when she had developed such a dark side. A grieving widow was preferable to a pitiful divorcee. Hot tears spilled onto her face but not because of the divorce or his infidelity. Those tears had dried up weeks ago. But for the shame of wishing John dead - the man she loved, with whom she had shared the past thirty years.

Katie had watched John change. Desperate to re-kindle his youth and terrified by his own mortality, compounded by the shock of losing a friend to a heart attack, he'd indulged in self-gratification—fast cars and beautiful young women. Katie had tried to ignore it as a phase, even attempting to reassure him by putting a spark in their marriage. It hadn't helped.

When her suggestions of marriage counselling were met with contempt, she sought counselling alone. It seemed she was always alone these days, except for Buddy-Boy, the three-year-old white fur ball of a dog usually curled up warmly on her feet. The counsellor advised her to stand up for herself and tell John to give up the women or else. Or else what? She didn't know. Had she pushed him into the arms of yet another thirty-year-old? Had the counselling changed her? She didn't like being bitter and vindictive. Wishing someone dead was not the real Katie. She wanted to be her old self again, happy, caring and loving but, except for Buddy-Boy, she had no one to love. The kids had flown the nest. Melanie, a botanist, was living in the wilds of Peru studying trees and Ben... well, keeping him on the straight-and-narrow was still a challenge. John said Ben was a free spirit and to leave him alone.

She worried about Ben.

John had settled in a modern downtown condo loft not big enough to swing a cat in, but that was the modern trend for young professionals. He could claim *professional* as a solicitor but at fifty-five, young he was not. She felt sorry for him; new neighbours looked at him with amusement, old friends shook their heads in disbelief—although, she suspected some of his male friends envied him.

John was happy. Katie was not.

The house echoed with emptiness now. The furniture, ornaments and paintings were unchanged John had left everything, but the place was sterile, empty of the important things—love and laughter.

Katie had chosen to be a stay at-home mum. She had

no interest in being a career woman; wife and mother was her career. Financially, they hadn't needed a second income and Katie had wanted to be home for the kids, bake apple pies for John and entertain friends. Dinner parties were the Saunders' signature, both in the neighbourhood and with the law partners. Although attractive, Katie had always been quiet and mousy but John had enough vitality for them both; a complementary combination of introvert and extrovert, or that's what she had thought. She had been wrong. And now, without John, the friends had disappeared. Friends and acquaintances from the law practice were understandable, but Katie's women friends from the neighbourhood, *that,* she did not understand.

Two exceptions were Judy Clayton and Phil Williams. She had met Judy when they were both pregnant with their sons and she'd been her best friend for the thirty plus years since. Sadly, Judy had moved away from the neighbourhood when her husband ran off with a wealthy older woman. The divorce had strengthened their already strong friendship. The other person was a tall, handsome young bachelor living amid suburban families and the subject of much gossip. Phil was an unlikely friend, but he'd been the only person on Autumn Road that had shown Katie any kindness or empathy.

Buddy-Boy gave a soft woof, but stayed at her feet. Katie looked up from the letter as a familiar voice called, "Knock, knock! Is anyone home?"

Katie brushed the tears from her face and patted her hair. *Not that it makes any difference,*she thought.

"Phil, come in. I'm sorry, I was miles away. I just received this." Katie pushed the letter into his hand, determined not to cry as Phil had already witnessed too many tears. "Have a seat.

I'll make tea, or would you prefer coffee?" she called from the kitchen.

"Tea's fine. So, it's official. How do you feel?"

"I'm fine. I'm over it," she yelled into the lounge, only to see Phil leaning against the kitchen doorway, his arms crossed.

"You don't look fine."

Katie shrugged and coughed away tears that stuck in the back of her throat. "I'm okay. I can get on with life now." Katie gave a tortured grin. "If I had a life. I don't know what to do. My life was John and the kids and they're gone. It's just Bud and I now." She leaned over and patted the dog. Buddy put his head to one side, his gentle eyes fixed on Katie.

"You need a purpose. Have you considered going back to school or getting a job?"

"This may sound shocking but I've never thought beyond the kids, except maybe we would travel and retire somewhere. I'll need to work, eventually." She gave a sharp laugh. "I'll be fifty-one at my next birthday and instead of retirement I'm looking for work. At least the court ordered John to pay alimony for three years, giving me a chance to train for a career and get a job."

"So, why don't you?" he said bluntly and smiled to soften his words.

"What skills do I have? Raising kids, sewing, cooking and entertaining are not exactly sought after corporate career skills. And going back to college with a bunch of kids younger than my own children is not appealing. I can't even use a computer beyond email and shopping on Amazon."

"You are bright, intelligent and could learn all kind of skills if you put your mind to it. What about teaching people how to entertain? No one in the neighbourhood can come close to your dinner parties. I can teach you some basic computer skills or you could go to night school. Most of the evening students are older people in the work force."

Katie didn't answer. As a professor at the college, Phil was enthusiastic about teaching and learning, which made her feel cornered and inadequate. She couldn't explain why, although leaving the house and meeting people scared her because she thought she would look like a fool. Everybody knew how to use a computer and nobody cooked anymore. She could never stand in front of a bunch of people and teach. What was Phil thinking? *I thought he was a friend. Some friend...*

"Katie, talk to me. What's wrong? I've upset you."

"No, its me. I feel raw. I can't plan for the future right now. Phil, I'm sorry but I need to be alone. Can we talk another time?"

Phil frowned. "Of course, but Katie are you sure you're all right?"

Katie gave a weak smile, "Honestly, I'm fine. I just need to be alone."

"O…k…ay," Phil said slowly and hesitated, "if you're sure. I'll drop by tomorrow."

Katie led him to the door and closed it. She cleared away the still full teacups. He hadn't even had time to drink his tea. *Is there something wrong with me? Pushing away a good friend who only wants to help.*

She loved entertaining but the idea of teaching strangers how to do it was frightening. It was different when she was hosting; she felt confident and in control, making her guests comfortable and feeding them good food. Was it even possible to turn entertaining into a skill?

The old grandfather clock chimed the hour. "Seven o'clock,"

she said aloud. "Too early to go to bed." She flipped the TV on and scrolled through the channels and then switched it off. Pulling the soft afghan up to her chin, Katie rested her head on the cushion, staring at the rain droplets trickling down the patio window. Buddy jumped up and snuggled up at her feet.

Ring! Ring! She sat up, startled, drunk with sleep. Who was calling in the middle of the night? Fumbling for the light, she realized she was on the couch and it was evening. The call display flashed Brianna Porter. Katie groaned, Brianna was the last person she wanted to talk to but the phone kept ringing.

"Hi Brianna. It's late. Can I call you tomorrow?"

Brianna lived opposite Katie. She was a self-absorbed young woman in her thirties, who didn't listen well and ignored Katie's request. "I'm popping over," Brianna said in her usual blunt fashion. "I have some exciting news." Katie heard the phone click and the doorbell ring simultaneously. Of course, so like Brianna, she'd called from her mobile.

"My, that was fast," Katie said, opening the front door. "Come in."

Brianna pushed passed Katie, high heels clicking on the hardwood floors. Katie glanced down at her fluffy slippers. Brianna folded the crumpled afghan and laid it across the back of the couch before she sat down.

"What can I do for you?" Katie snapped, forcing a grin.

"It's what I can do for you." Brianna, in a smart designer skirt and silk blouse, said with a self-satisfied smug. Katie had a strong desire to slap the smugness away but refrained. "I was coming home from work, late as usual, and bumped into Phil leaving here this evening and I asked how you were doing. He said he thought you needed a job, something to do. I have just the job for you." The smugness was becoming offensive and Katie's anger threshold, usually high, was reaching the breaking point. How could Phil betray her trust and discuss her business with such a nosey-parker? Brianna was the nastiest gossip on the street!

"Phil had no right to discuss our conversation. I'm not looking for a job. John is providing for me." Katie felt the familiar lump in her throat and willed herself not to cry in front of Brianna.

"It's not just about money, although I fail to see why you would want a man's support. Don't you want to be independent?" Brianna stared, waiting for an answer.

"Maybe," Katie replied. *Actually,* she thought *I have no desire for independence but I no longer have a choice.*

"Becket Marketing Ltd, the firm where I work, has a job opening that would suit you. Assistant to the events coordinator. It's perfect!"

"I know nothing about events."

"Of course you do. Planning events and entertaining clients. It would be like planning dinner parties every week and you are an expert." She smiled. "There are few people I envy but I envy your talent for entertaining."

"Are those skills the same?" Katie wasn't ready to admit it but she was interested and Brianna's compliment was praise indeed. Perhaps this was something she could do. She always felt so good planning, cooking and entertaining. "I'll think about it."

"Don't be too long, I'll recommend you to Sylvie, she's the coordinator. Can you give me a copy of your resume?"

Now it was Katie's turn to stare. She'd never written a resume and was embarrassed to admit she didn't know how.

Brianna shrugged and added, "Not to worry, if you don't have one, I'll put something together and write you a letter of reference. Sylvie trusts my opinion."

"Okay."

"I'll call tomorrow with a time for an interview." Brianna's eyes scanned Katie's pull-on polyester slacks and floral embroidered sweatshirt. "Do you have a tailored business suit? ...For the interview, of course."

Katie shook her head. She'd never owned a business suit. She had nice dresses and jackets for going out with John but she doubted they would pass as a business suit.

"Never mind. I'll take you shopping. I can leave work early tomorrow and pick you up at three. Now I must run, I have work to finish."

Katie waved goodbye and wondered what had just happened. Brianna had just taken over.

The boot of Brianna's BMW clicked open and Katie lifted out three fancy carrier bags. A flash of excitement tugged at her; she had never shopped in such fancy boutique stores, nor had she ever spent so much money. It was liberating. Brianna had taken her to dinner and given Katie advice about the upcoming interview with Sylvie.

Katie, beaming with gratitude gave Brianna a hug. "Thank you for all your help. I couldn't have done this without you. Will I see you tomorrow at the interview?"

"No, I've already spoken to Sylvie. I have a big off-site meeting tomorrow. Good luck!"

"Thanks." Katie ran across the road just as Phil rounded the corner onto Autumn Road. She waved shopping bags in the air as he pulled into his driveway and five minutes later Phil was on her doorstep.

"Phil come in. What do you think of my new outfit?"

She pulled out a navy-blue pencil slim skirt and tailored jacket from one bag and a soft pale, leaf-green blouse from another. Holding the outfit against her body, she tried to slide her feet into the navy high heel shoes and almost fell over. Phil caught her just in time and they laughed.

"Very smart, but the falling off your shoes might not give the right impression." The comment prompted more laughing. "It is so good to hear you laugh again. I'm surprised but Brianna has turned out to be a friend. I'd still be cautious, though. Don't be fooled by her kindness. She may have an ulterior motive."

"I have to admit Brianna has surprised me too. Most of the street has ignored me since John left. It's nice to have a friend."

"People don't like change. I think the women are afraid you'll run off with their husbands. They'll get over it."

"I hope so but in times like this you learn who your friends are." Katie clapped her hands and her voice raised an octave. "Can you believe I'm going for a job interview tomorrow and that is all Brianna's doing?"

"How do you feel about working? Last time we spoke you didn't want to work."

"Nervous but I might as well take this opportunity."

"A wise choice. It's time to put John in the past. I'm proud of you." Phil squeezed her hand. "I must go. I'll see you tomorrow."

Katie laid the business suit over the chair and plopped down onto the couch, feeling a sense of euphoria. She was starting a new life.

Two

Elation to Defeat

*K*atie watched as the numbers on the bedside clock flipped to 6 a.m. She'd been awake since five and in the last hour she had changed her mind about going to the interview four times. Her stomach was in knots and her heart vibrated so hard she couldn't breathe, her head rambling with thoughts. *Am I having a panic attack? Wouldn't that look good in an interview! Pull yourself together Katie Saunders and get out of bed.*

Katie swung her feet to the floor, switched the light on and smiled at the navy-blue business suit hanging on the wardrobe door. "So… John Saunders what do you think of your mousy wife now?"

Katie bounded downstairs with Buddy at her heels. Sensing her excitement, he wagged his curly tail and gave Katie expectant looks. She picked him up in her arms; at fifteen pounds he was a perfect size for hugs. "Being a dog must be wonderful. Here you are, all happy but you have no idea what's happening. Or do you just want to chase squirrels?" She put him on the floor, filled the coffee pot and opened the back door, shivering from a blast of cold air. The autumn wind was blowing wet leaves in circles and driving the rain into the house. Buddy looked at the rain, turned back into the kitchen and sat on his bed. He gave Katie a look of are-you-crazy-expecting-me-to-go-out-in-that. Katie laughed and squatted down, petting his soft lamb-like fur.

The coffee pot sputtered to a stop and she poured a coffee, studying the information Brianna had given her about Becket Marketing and the events they planned. She stopped reading as her stomach knotted and the coffee churned. Nauseous, fear gripped her whole body. How could she go to an interview in this state? Buddy's wet nose on her leg startled her and forced away the negative thoughts. She picked him up again, rubbed his ears and kissed the top of his head. "Thanks Bud. I'm being silly, but this is so difficult. What if they don't like me?" As though he understood every word, Buddy rested his head against her chest and she could feel his energy. "You're right, Bud, I can do this." Buddy jumped down and stared at the backdoor, his way of saying he needed to go out. Katie opened the door, surprised at the change in the weather. The wind had calmed to a pleasant breeze and a glimmer of sunshine shone on the morning horizon. She waited for Buddy to come in and ran upstairs to get ready.

Katie grinned in front of the long mirror. The transformation was amazing. She hardly recognized the woman staring back at her from the mirror. The suit was perfect, the heels, higher than she normally wore, gave her five foot two inches an extra boost. She'd debated whether to wear her hair up or down and left it down. It suited her impish face and took off a few years. "Business-like but friendly," she said to her reflection.

It was a twenty-minute drive from Autumn Road to Milton, a typical English market town, populated with businesses escaping the rat race and the high rent of the big cities. Katie turned into the parking lot of Becket Marketing, relieved to find one visitor parking space. The car radio announced BBC's 9:30 news and she sighed, half an hour to wait until her 10 a.m. interview. Searching for something to do to counter her nerves, she pulled down the sun visor and checked her make-up in the mirror, distracted by the reflection of a bookstore. Browsing for ten minutes would occupy her mind. *No,* she thought, *I'll lose track of time.* By the time she decided, it was already 9:45.

The receptionist gave her a corporate smile and asked Ms. Saunders to take a seat while she contacted Ms. Vickers. *Ms not Mrs. I like that*Katie thought.*It removes me from being John's wife.* She declined a coffee. Her hands were shaking, and she didn't need coffee down her silk blouse.

Ms. Vickers appeared with her hand outstretched. "Good morning Ms. Saunders." They shook hands. "Thanks for coming. Follow me, please"

Katie followed like an obedient dog. Ms. Vickers wore the corporate uniform, grey suit and black, heeled pumps, short neat blonde hair and just enough make-up to look smart. Despite Katie's extra heel height, Ms. Vickers towered over her. *She must be six feet tall,*Katie thought, *and skinny.*

The interview passed quickly; Ms. Vickers asked a few

questions and referred to the resume as being just what she was looking for, which surprised Katie. Her college diploma was only in domestic science and a subsequent certificate, in design, old and not relevant. Ms. Vickers was most interested in the events planning; Katie assumed this was Brianna's interpretation of Katie's dinner party planning. After she gave impressive answers to the final questions, Ms. Vickers asked Katie to wait while she contacted Mr. Becket. Katie had the impression that if Mr. Becket approved, the job was hers.

Ms. Vickers left the room and Katie wanted to pinch herself; she could hardly believe this was happening. She glanced around the windowless room, furnished with highly polished wood furniture and upholstered chairs. The walls were full of photos of various events. A few had famous people holding champagne glasses. She recognized the prime minister in one and a couple of film stars but most were of local groups from Derby and Nottingham. She stood up to examine an older photo, thinking the man looked like Winston Churchill. Suddenly the door slammed and Katie almost jumped out of her skin. A man in a pinstriped business suit, of average build and with thinning grey hair, walked into the room.

"I didn't mean to startle you. I'm Graham Becket and that gentleman shaking hands with Winston Churchill is my grandfather, the founder of this company." He motioned for Katie to sit down and took the chair opposite her. "Sylvie was impressed with your interview and Brianna highly recommends you for the position."

"Thank you." Katie's eyes dropped to her feet, uncomfortable with the compliments.

"I've read your resume and I have a few questions. You haven't worked for a while, have you? Why is that?"

Katie didn't lie well. No matter what Brianna had put in her resume, she had to be honest. "No, I chose to stay at home to raise my family. Planning social events and entertaining is something I've been doing for the last twenty-five years and I do it well. Now I'm div...," she cleared her throat, "Now my kids are grown, I can bring those skills into the workforce." Katie looked down at her feet again. "Mr. Becket, I am a fast learner."

His head nodded and he grinned slightly. "Please call me Graham. It is refreshing to meet someone who is not afraid to be honest. I tire of the young with their sense of entitlement." He leaned forward. "Are you married?"

Katie was suddenly uncomfortable. Graham's question was inappropriate but she answered. "Recently divorced."

"You'll do nicely. Sylvie will give you all the details. Welcome aboard Katie." He patted her hand and left the room.

Two weeks in, Katie had already settled into her job. She struggled with the computer but did well talking to clients and planning the details for events. Sylvie was a good teacher and they made a great team. Brianna had been correct; planning a large event wasn't much different from a dinner party. She saw little of Brianna. As an account manager she was often out of the office or out of town at events.

On Saturday morning, Katie hooked the leash onto Buddy's collar and, much to Buddy's disappointment, put him in the back of the car—Buddy hated car rides and showed his displeasure by whining.

"Bud, stop whining. I'm taking you to Springsville. You love walking by the canal and we're meeting Judy for lunch." She glanced in the rearview mirror as Buddy's head moved from side to side. He recognized the names and put his head on his paws, reducing the whining to whimpering.

Katie drove into Springsville, turned down Marina Lane and parked at Bob's Marina. She opened the car boot and pulled on a pair of Wellington boots to protect her feet from the mud and puddles along the canal towpath. Taking a deep breath, she relished the sweet-smelling autumn leaves and fresh rain on the grass with a hint of canal water. It always felt damp and chilly in November but the rain had held off and the sun kept peeking through the clouds.

The morning silence was broken by the lapping water as the narrowboats rocked gently at their moorings, interspersed by the occasional quack from mallards paddling between the boats. There was even the familiar plop of an otter going off for a morning swim. Katie stood still with Buddy at her feet and stared at the colourful canal basin. The narrowboats, once working barges hauling coal and goods up and down the British canal system, had transformed into brightly painted holiday boats. The interiors had modern mini kitchens and bathrooms, sleeping cabins and elaborate lounges. They had names like *Journey's End*, *Daisy-May* and Katie's favourite, *Tranquil Days*. The name mirrored her mood every time she came to Springsville, tranquil and happy, especially out of season. She instinctively understood the narrowboats anticipation as they rested, waiting for families to return in the spring.

"Okay, Bud, are you ready?" Buddy stood up, wagging his tail, and led Katie to the towpath.

Walks along this path had been a great comfort to Katie when she had discovered John's affairs. The quietness allowed her to think and put things into perspective. Today, she thought about Becket Marketing. She was pleased with her accomplishments and the new sense of self-worth—no longer an extension of John. This last thought pleased her, even surprised her, as she had always been quite happy being John's wife. And, now she was entering a new and very different life, she felt tightness in her stomach as her thoughts shifted to her job. *Is the corporate world what I really want? The superficial niceties annoy me. All those false smiles. How can we help you, meaning how can we make money from you? It isn't Beckets in particular, although Graham Becket worries me. It's the whole corporate culture. I don't belong.*

Buddy stopped to sniff an interesting clump of grass and Katie waited patiently, leaning against the stone bridge. She watched a lone narrowboat, painted bright green with a red roof and gold trim, chug under the bridge. A little brown terrier sat at the bow and barked as the man at the tiller waved and yelled "Good morning. Beautiful day!"

Katie waved back, "It's a perfect day!" Buddy barked his greeting to the terrier and trotted ahead of Katie, keeping pace with the narrowboat until a man with a large dog, an Alsatian, bounded towards them. Buddy stopped dead in his tracks, turned to look at Katie and ran back to her heels, barking ferociously.

The man nodded and said, "Lovely day." He glanced at the barking Buddy. "He's attempting to protect you. Rex wouldn't hurt a fly unless someone tried to hurt me."

Katie looked at Rex. "I think Buddy has small-dog syndrome and I'm not comfortable around big dogs. He senses my fear. Rex is a fine looking animal. Good day to you, sir!" The man nodded and Katie could have sworn that Rex lifted his head and sneered at poor Bud. She couldn't help but laugh. If dogs could talk, she suspected Buddy would chastise her for laughing.

"Okay, Buddy, time to go back to the car, clean up and meet Judy." They had walked further than Katie realized. It was almost noon when they reached the car.

She removed her muddy boots, replacing them with her shoes. She looked at the not very white Buddy and pulled a large beach towel from her bag. Buddy's feet and legs were dark brown and his underbelly dripped with muddy water. She wrapped him in the towel and rubbed his muddy chin and belly, leaving his paws until last. She wiped them gently since he hated it as much as car rides. Once she finished, he gave her a lick, jumped down and shook himself.

"Well, you look more brown than white but you'll do." Katie grabbed her handbag and closed the boot.

"That's why I chose Arthur. He's already brown."

Katie spun around and came face to face with a man in his fifties, flashing a generous and kind smile that filled his round face. "We meet again."

"We do?" Katie frowned.

"We met this morning as I floated under the stone bridge. I moor my boat here." He pointed to the green and gold narrowboat and Katie read the name painted in gold letters on the bow of the boat: *Tranquil Days.*

"Oh yes. Sorry, I didn't recognize you without your boat." She laughed. "Oh dear, that sounded weird."

"Not at all. My boat is a big part of my life, summer and winter."

"Of all the boats here, my favourite name is *Tranquil Days.*"

"Thank you. That boat has seen me through tough times."

"I understand. Walking along the towpath helped me deal

with…" Katie didn't know what to say. She was about to tell this stranger her life story. "As you say, tough times."

"I have to leave but do you come here often?" He burst out laughing. "That has to be the worst line ever. Before I embarrass myself anymore, I will bid you good day."

"Often on a Saturday morning," she called after him. "Nice to meet you."

He waved and called Arthur who was chasing Buddy around the picnic table. They jumped in their car and drove away.

"Come, Buddy!" Katie clipped the leash back on Buddy's collar and they walked across to Mary's Bakery and Café.

Three

Springsville

*K*atie breathed in the delicious aromas coming from the café. She was dying for a good cup of coffee and Mary's was the best. Her tummy rumbled. The long walk had given her an appetite. Buddy led her past the empty tables on the verandah, November being a little chilly to eat outside, and they headed for the area called Dog Moorings. She always thought it was such a lovely idea, indicative of the kind of people the owners, Mary and Bob Bingham, were. A series of hooks for dog leashes were attached under the sign and two big bowls of fresh water were ready for thirsty dogs. Buddy lapped water, before curling up for a nap. He was unusually alone today. Katie had expected to see Sam and Lily, Judy's Golden retrievers. They usually walked across the fields as Judy couldn't keep the retrievers out of the water if they were off leash. She glanced around and then saw Judy waving from a prime window table from inside the café. When it was too cold to sit outside, this table was second best and allowed them to watch the boats and the dogs.

"Good to see you," they said in unison as they wrapped their arms around each other. Judy already had a coffee so Katie ordered herself a latte and two of the usual chicken specials with salad.

"Where are the dogs?" Katie asked.

"Lily cut her paw on Thursday, the bleeding was awful. The vet thinks she stepped on a piece of glass, thankfully, it wasn't as bad as it looked. He bandaged it and said to keep the dressing dry for a few days. Poor Lily has one of those enormous collar things to stop her chewing the dressing so no walks for either of them. Sam isn't at all happy but I can't take Sam and leave Lily."

"Ah poor Lily, and Max must be chaffing at the bit. So how are you doing?"

"Good, the new project in Derby is coming along fine. Changing the subject, who's the guy you were talking to?"

"He owns a boat here. I don't know him but we spoke in passing." Katie grinned remembering his embarrassment.

"He's cute," Judy said, "Why the grin?"

"Are you trying to hook me up with a stranger? Aren't we too old for that?" They both giggled.

"Tell me, how is the job going?" Judy leaned forward waiting for Katie's reply.

"It's okay."

"What's changed? You sounded so enthusiastic on the phone."

"The job is going well and surprise, surprise I can do the work. I'm even enjoying it but I'm not sure I'm cut out for the corporate thing." Katie took a breath, hesitated, but said nothing.

"Katie Saunders, I have known you for thirty years and something is wrong. Is John badgering you or has Brianna shown you her true colours?"

"I haven't heard from John since the final papers arrived and I'm over him. What do you mean about Brianna? She's been kind, taking me shopping and getting me this job. I never see her at work though."

"Are you going to tell me or not?"

"Okay, I'm probably overreacting but Graham Becket is... shall we say, familiar? I mentioned it to Sylvie, and she brushed it off, saying not to read anything in to it, but then added, don't encourage him."

"What does he do?"

"It's hard to pinpoint. He appears kind and empathetic, he comments on me being alone and hurt by the divorce. He doesn't say or do the same things to Sylvie or anyone else in the office except maybe Brianna. I thought something was going on between them but its work; they work together with the VIP clients. Sylvie told me he works hard to pay for his kids in college, so he's married."

Judy frowned. "That doesn't mean much, except he's not getting it at home. Can you describe his actions?"

"He pats my hand. At least it's not my behind. If I'm alone in the office, he makes an excuse to come into my cubicle. He sidles up much too close and is always complimenting me, my hair, my clothes and even my legs. I changed my wardrobe and wore slacks and Sylvie told me to wear skirts in the office. He has trouble raising his eyes above my breasts but he does that with all the woman, especially the young office girls who don't have the sense to cover up cleavage."

"Dear Katie, you are so naïve. Listen, this is not right. It's sexual harassment. Tell him to move away when he gets too close, and that touching is inappropriate. When he stares at your breasts, tell him 'eyes up here' and point to your face."

"I'm afraid to say anything."

"If you don't, he will get worse. Remember, I work in a man's world and there are few women in engineering. I have had to slap a lot of hands, and some faces, as my colleagues attempted to touch me inappropriately. I don't tolerate snide sexist remarks. I had to be quite the bitch to get them to listen. It took a while but now I'm treated with respect."

"I couldn't do that!"

"Someone needs to set an example and clearly it won't be Sylvie or Brianna."

Katie sighed and muttered, "I understand. I'll think about it." She couldn't do any of the things Judy suggested but ignoring it was not a solution. Talking about it had made her aware that she feared Graham Becket.

Relieved when the waitress placed lunch on the table, Katie changed the subject. "I had an email from Melanie yesterday. She is coming home next weekend. Well, not exactly home. She's speaking at Nottingham University but will stay with me for a couple of nights."

"Something to look forward to. It's been, what, a year since she was home?" Judy pointed to her plate. "This is so good but homemade bread is so bad for you. It's no wonder I can't lose weight."

"Why do you want to lose weight? You look good as you are. At least you don't have a D cup and, as my mother would say, childbearing hips. It doesn't matter what I do, I can't lose weight."

"I wish I had more of your figure. I'm flat chested and square. But like you, no matter how I diet, my shape stays the same. But I love good food so let's eat up." They sat in a comfortable silence and finished their meal.

"I love this village, it's so peaceful," Katie said, staring at the colourful narrowboats. She imagined the gentle movements were giant knitting needles, stitching the boats into an intricate pattern and producing an amazing picture. "You know, Judy, I could live here and entertain. Have summer BBQs, organize doggie walks and hikes all along the canal."

"Now that sounds more like you than Becket Marketing. Why don't you?"

Buddy barked and Katie jumped up to check on him. "Oh, it's raining. Time to leave before Buddy gets soaked. Come to the house?"

"I'd love to but I have things to do. I'll call you," Judy added, as they walked to their cars.

Too tired to whine, Buddy slept for the forty-five minute drive to Autumn Road while Katie mulled over the morning's conversation with Judy. She had confirmed Graham's behaviour as being inappropriate but she wasn't sure is it was sexual harassment. She didn't like his advances but did she have the courage to tell him? She shook her head. Confrontation was not her strong point and she would risk getting fired. The job was important to her. Pulling into the driveway, she pressed the garage remote, drove in and turned off the engine. The best thing to do was to avoid him. She stared through the opening as the garage door closed. *Am I seeing things?* She could have sworn she saw Graham Becket going into Brianna's house. *That's odd* she thought *I guess they are working on a big job. I can't think of any new projects. At least none that require weekend work.*

Buddy ran into the back garden, barking at a squirrel that had had the audacity to collect fallen acorns from under the oak tree. Katie laughed. "Come inside Bud. The squirrel needs a stash of acorns for the winter."

Curious, Katie peered through the front window, expecting to see Graham Becket's car but Brianna's BMW sat in the driveway. Perhaps she was seeing things?

Monday morning, Katie took Buddy for an extra-long walk, to compensate for leaving him alone all day. She loved quiet early mornings as the night sky turned dark blue and the moon faded. Fellow dog walkers always had a cheery 'good morning.' Katie had a spring to her step, looking forward to going to work, to having a purpose in life.

Not paying attention to her surroundings Katie watched the moon disappear as the glow of sunrise speckled through the bare trees. Almost too late, she spotted the approaching car. She yanked the leash, pulling Buddy to her heels and stared at the driver as the car whizzed by. "Graham?" she said out loud, "That was Graham Becket driving that car." She patted Buddy and added. "I doubt it was a business weekend—you're having an affair with Brianna." Katie wasn't sure if she was excited or disgusted by the scandal. Disgusted was appropriate. She shuddered, wondering why any woman would want that creep. As she approached her house, she glanced across the street. Brianna's garage door gaped open and the BMW was no longer in the driveway but on the street. Under her breath she whispered, "I guess he hid his car in the garage."

Sylvie sat at her desk sipping her morning coffee when Katie arrived. "Morning, Katie. Glad you're early. I want you to take over the Nottingham Home Exhibition." Sylvie handed Katie a three-page list and explained each item. "I know the work is new to you so follow the list and ask questions." She looked Katie in the eye. "Right, Katie? There are no wrong questions."

"Right. Thank you. You are a good teacher."

"I can't emphasize enough that detail is very important when planning an event and the bigger the event, the more detail." Katie nodded. She admired Sylvie's ability to organize the tiniest detail; an attribute Katie thought she lacked.

"Graham wants the preliminary report, a condensed version of this list, for the meeting this afternoon. I talked to him this morning. His meeting in London was a success this weekend. Looks as though we might have another exhibition for next year. He said he'd be in later as his train from London was late last night."

"I saw him when I was walking Buddy this morn…." Katie stopped talking, sorry that the words had sprung from her mouth without thinking.

"Whatever you saw, forget it, if you want to keep your job."

"I guess I was mistaken. It was dark."

"Good girl, Katie. I like you, but be careful or your naivety will get you into trouble."

Katie grinned nervously. She didn't like what she heard. Sylvie knew of the affair and was okay with it but Katie wasn't. How could Brianna do that? Graham had a wife and children. *I guess I am naïve or I know how infidelity hurts.*

Sylvie smiled and switched the conversation back to work. "I'd like you to study this list and break it up under headings. I've sent you the document. It won't take long to type up the condensed version. Make twelve copies for the meeting and I'd like you to attend, as an observer. I'll see you later. I have to meet a client."

Eager to learn as much as she could, Katie immersed herself in the list, looking up things and compiling the report on the computer. She was improving but her typing was still slow. She almost jumped off her chair when Graham's voice boomed into the cubicle. "Hard at work, I see. Is that the report for this afternoon's meeting?"

"Yes," Katie said as Graham moved closer. "Where's Sylvie?"

"She's with a client." Katie could feel his hot breath on her neck and as he reached to touch her shoulder, she jumped up from her desk, his eyes fixed on her breast.

"Graham, this behaviour is inappropriate and my eyes are up here, not in my chest." Katie held her breath. She smiled, hearing Judy cheering in her head.

"How dare you!" His face turned purple with rage, his hands clenched into fists.

Katie backed away, afraid he might hit her. "I think you need to leave. I have work to do." She sat heavily in her chair as he left, allowing the pent-up air to escape. Her heart wouldn't stop thumping. She tried to type, but she kept hitting the wrong keys; her hands shook so much. She needed a distraction to bring her heart back to a normal pace. She picked up the phone and called Judy.

"Katie, what's up?"

"I need help. I told Graham to get lost," she whispered into the phone.

"Well done, Katie. Okay, deep breaths, think about Melanie coming home, anything to take your mind off of it."

Judy chattered away for about ten minutes. Katie couldn't

remember the conversation but she felt better when she hung up and remembered that Judy promised to drop by the house after work.

Sylvie walked in as she was printing off the reports. "Good work, Katie. Take an early lunch and I'll see you back here at 1 p.m."

"Thanks." Katie ran out of the office and began walking. The exercise calmed her and helped her to think. Her shaking hands told her the Graham incident had unnerved her and, despite Judy's reassurance, she worried about the consequences. Judy said to think of something pleasant like her daughter but Katie hadn't said how disappointed she was that Melanie spent almost all her time with friends. Thinking of her daughter didn't help.

Milton was a pleasant historic market town but the old narrow streets were congested with cars and trucks that filled the country air with diesel fumes. It spoiled the old town feel and was not ideal for a leisurely stroll. She would have preferred to walk in Springsville, breathing in the scent of autumn leaves, Michaelmas Daisies and Mary's fresh brewed coffee. *Why* she wondered *is Springsville so appealing? Because I'm comfortable there. I love the rich environment and uncomplicated people. If it wasn't for the long commute, I could live in Springsville.*

The old town clock chimed the half hour and she smiled to herself. She had found something to take her mind off her shaking hands and thumping heart. The pain in her heeled feet told her she had walked a long way and she groaned, knowing that if she didn't run back to the office, she would be late.

Four

Life Changing Decisions

Katie followed Sylvie into the boardroom and smiled at Brianna who glared back. Katie frowned. *Why is Brianna upset?*

"Good afternoon, everyone!" Sylvie said standing at Katie's side. "Most of you have met Katie, my new assistant. I hope you don't mind but I asked her to sit in and observe the meeting as she learns the ropes."

"Get her out of here! This is an executive meeting." Graham's voice vibrated the air in the room.

"I'm sorry Graham, I don't understand…" Sylvie stopped as Graham stared at her.

Katie stood up, glancing at the witch's grin that spread across Brianna's face and the raised eyebrow as Katie left the room. Katie puzzled over Brianna's look but was aware that Graham was punishing her for challenging his sexist behaviour. Perhaps Judy's advice was not the best.

Not able to concentrate, Katie shuffled papers on her desk and listened for the boardroom door to open. It was four o'clock before Sylvie came out of the boardroom and headed for her office. Without stopping, she yelled, "My office now!" Katie followed. "Close the door and take a seat." Sylvie let out a long sigh, "Katie, what did you do?" Her voice softened and her attitude changed. Graham is furious with you but he wouldn't say why and Brianna is accusing you of flirting with him."

"Flirting! No! The opposite happened. I told him I didn't like his behaviour and to stop looking at my breasts, or words to that effect."

"That explains Graham. A word of advice. Keep your distance and never challenge him. It's wrong but if you want to keep your job, get used to it. With any luck, he'll overlook it this time."

"What if I don't want to 'get used to it'?"

"Then find another job. It's that simple. Why would Brianna accuse you of flirting?"

"I don't know. I saw Graham leaving her place Monday morning." Katie hesitated. "What I didn't tell you was that I saw him going into her house on Saturday."

"Katie, you are so naïve. Graham is having an affair with Brianna. The business trips they take together never result in sales. I didn't know he was going to her house though. You live near Brianna?"

"Yes. Across the street."

"Ah, I'd have thought they'd be more careful. The affair is common knowledge in the office but nobody talks about it."

Sylvie's office door burst open and Graham marched in with Brianna behind him. "Brianna just told me that you are spreading rumours implying I'm having an affair with you.

What do you have to say about that, Katie?" He poked a finger at her.

"I never said any such thing! Perhaps you are covering something up?"

For the second time that afternoon, Graham shouted. "Get out of here!" and added, "You're fired! Deal with it, Sylvie."

Sylvie and Katie stared at the empty doorway as Graham and Brianna marched back to their respective offices. Heads popped up over the cubicles. The whole office had heard.

"I'm sorry, but I have no choice. I'll miss you. We could have been a great team."

Too stunned to answer, Katie stood motionless, trying to figure out what had just happened.

"I wish I could say he will change his mind, but he won't."

As though she hadn't heard Sylvie, she said, "I would never have an affair. Now the whole office thinks I'm... the other woman, a whore." The injustice made her angry. "How could anyone think I'd do something like that?"

"I suspect Brianna made up the story to divert suspicion." Sylvie closed the door as nosy heads dropped behind screens. "Katie, this is the real world. Sexual harassment happens in every workplace. I admire your courage to tell Graham that his behaviour was inappropriate but the results are what you see."

"Why do you let it continue?"

"I'm a single mum with two young kids. I need the job. He pays well and I love my work, so I put up with it. This might sound odd, but since he started the affair with Brianna, he eased up on the harassment. And then you arrived."

"Me? I did nothing."

"But he fancied you. Your innocence appealed to him; newly

30

divorced and vulnerable. That would not please Brianna."

"I see what you mean."

"I'm sorry. Will you be all right for money?"

"I liked working with you but the corporate culture is not for me. I couldn't work with someone like Graham anyway. Money is fine. My ex is supporting me for a while."

"I'll have payroll cut you a cheque and I'll call you when it's ready. Gather your belongings and I'll walk you to your car. Are you okay to drive? I can drive you home if you like."

Picking up the photos of Melanie and Ben—the only personal things on her desk—she pushed them in her handbag saying, "I'm fine but thank you." She and Sylvie walked through the office to the parking lot.

"Give me a hug, Katie Saunders. You may have done the office a favour. Graham will be careful for a while. Good luck and take care."

The drive to Autumn Road took longer than usual because of heavy traffic. She'd felt numb when she got in the car but all kinds of feelings were beginning to erupt. She wanted to get home. Her mobile rang and announced that Judy Clayton was calling.

"Hello, Judy."

"Where are you?"

"Oh gosh, sorry Judy. I forgot you were coming. I was late leaving the office and I'm stuck in traffic. Can you wait? I need to talk to you."

"I can wait. Is it Graham again?"

"Yes. He fired me."

"What!?"

"I'll tell you when I get home. I need to concentrate on driving."

Anger bubbled up like thick mud and teardrops perched on her bottom eyelid, ready to flow again. Determined not to give in to either tears or anger, she tried to change her thoughts. As soon as she pulled into her driveway and made eye contact with Judy though, she burst into angry tears. Judy put her arms around her, took her keys to unlock the front door, and led her to the sofa. They sat side by side and Buddy jumped on Katie's knee. She patted him as he looked up at her, resting his head on her chest, knowing something was wrong. Katie kissed his head and brushed her wet tears from his fur.

"Come, Buddy, you need to go out." She gave a weak smile. "At least Buddy will be happy I'm home all day."

Katie ordered pizza, opened a bottle of wine and related the events to Judy. It made a big difference having a friend to confide in and, by the end of the evening, they were laughing. Katie went to bed, embracing a sense of relief knowing she did not have to get up in the morning and pretend she was someone she wasn't.

Buddy wiggled his back into Katie as she stretched, counting the chimes as the grandfather clock struck eight. She shivered, feeling the cool morning. Buddy jumped off the bed and trotted downstairs. It took Katie a minute to gather her thoughts and, remembering yesterday, she rolled over, not wanting to get out of bed. An indignant 'woof' from Buddy prompted her to pull on her warm housecoat and open the back door. Buddy ran out, leaving footprints on the heavy white frost covering the lawn. She cursed, remembering she had left her car in the driveway. She hated scraping frost off the car but as she didn't have to go to work, she could just let it melt as the day got warmer. Buddy came in and sat by her feet. "I know you want a walk." At the word *walk* his tail thumped on the floor, his head at a cute angle he looked up. "How can I resist that sweet face?" She ran upstairs and pulled on grey sweat pants and a thick hoody. Hooking Buddy to his leash, they headed for the park. The sun had begun melting the frost, the air smelled fresh and cool and the trees engulfed in ice crystals looked pretty. Now and then, she heard a tinkling sound as a piece of ice hit the pavement—a magical moment.

As they walked back to the house, Phil jogged towards them. "Good morning! Is everything okay? You've usually left for work before I go for my morning run."

"Fine. I got fired yesterday."

"What happened? Did Brianna have anything to do with it?"

"The answer is yes and no. Do you have time for coffee after your run?"

"I told you to watch her. Coffee sounds great. I don't have classes until 11:30 today."

"Half an hour?"

Phil nodded yes, and jogged to the end of the street, disappearing around the corner.

Katie filled the coffee pot and took carrot muffins out of the freezer before going to shower and change. Wearing her comfortable pull-on trousers and warm loose-fitting fleece, she tied her hair in a ponytail and added lipstick but left her eyes and cheeks au-natural.

"Knock, knock, it's me. Ah, the coffee smells good."

"Come in, take a seat." Katie poured two big mugs of coffee. "Help yourself." She pointed to the muffins and a plate of fresh fruit on the kitchen table.

"So, what happened?" Phil asked, taking a bite of muffin.

"Um, these are good."

"I told Graham I didn't appreciate his sexual attitude and Brianna accused me of having an affair with Graham."

"Wow! He fired you for that? You can report him for wrongful dismissal, you know. Brianna is covering her butt!"

"Right on both counts."

"The college is very tough on sexual harassment. They have to be. We are dealing with young vulnerable students. You should report him."

"I couldn't do that. He'd make everyone's life hell. The others just put up with it, afraid for their jobs. With good reason."

"Will you look for another job or go back to school? The college has a variety of interesting programs. I can bring you a prospectus if you'd like."

"Maybe." She watched Phil stand up. His tight jogging suit clung to him and she felt her body stir. *He's very handsome* she thought.*Stop thinking that way. I'm not interested. Heavens, the ink on the divorce papers is hardly dry and he's years younger than me. Becket Marketing has been a bad influence on me.*

"I have to get moving, stuff to do before class. Thanks for the coffee and muffins."

Talking to herself as she pulled the vacuum to and fro on the clean carpet, Katie wondered what she could do with her time. "Maybe I'll cook Phil a nice dinner or better still, I'll have a dinner party. It'll be weird without John but I need to accept it and let the neighbours know I can still entertain. It'll be fun. They all enjoy my dinner parties."

Katie put the vacuum away and wrote an email inviting four couples and Phil, who evened up the numbers—usually because of Brianna, the only single woman on the street. Katie chuckled. It's interesting how we thought she was a career woman with no time for dating. For obvious reasons, Brianna was not on the guest list this time.

Comforted by the familiar, Katie sat at the kitchen table and planned the menu. *I'll make four courses*, she thought, *I'll prepare the favourites: avocado with shrimp, chicken a la Mum.* She laughed. The recipe came from her mother and had a French name she always forgot. John had teased her, calling it 'a la Mum'. A shiver of fear rippled along her spine. Was she capable of doing this without John? Her throat tightened and her eyes blurred but the tears didn't come. Something snapped and Katie sat up straight. "Enough! You're pathetic," she scolded. "John has gone and you have a new life." Her positive thoughts wavered. After all, she had been fired from her first job, making her wonder how well she really was doing. But she needed to push forward. Turning her attention back to Saturday night's menu, she had all the confidence in the world about cooking and entertaining. She added sweet kale salad to the main course and a light soup to start. Apple pie, an all-time favourite and sinful chocolate cake for dessert.

The menu planned, and the list complete, Katie picked up the shopping bags and drove to the butchers for fresh chicken and then on to the supermarket. She checked the food items in her cart and wandered along the wine aisle, trying to recognize wine labels. She had never paid attention to the wines John selected. She chose two red and two white wines with pretty labels.

For the next two days, Katie hummed her favourite Diana Krall jazz songs and listened to a little Mozart while she ironed linen napkins, hating paper ones. The white damask table cloth took ages to iron, but she didn't mind. She had a purpose. Next, she set the table for ten with the Royal Doulton china, silver cutlery and cut glass wine glasses. She was old fashioned. Few people had 'best' china these days, but she liked it and so did her guests.

Surprised that not everyone had replied to her invite, she picked up her iPhone and checked her messages. Phil had replied and so had Anne and Dave but nothing from the others. She sent out a quick reminder.

Katie liked to be organized when entertaining. Friday morning, she prepared as much of the food in advance as she could. She gave a big sigh and sat relaxing with a well-earned coffee while she checked email. She grinned at the screen. *Ah, good, replies at last.* The grin disappeared as she read Anne and Dave's email. An apology as something had come up and they couldn't make it. The other three delinquent couples replied with identical terse replies of 'sorry can't make it.' The words from people she called friends jumped off the screen and slapped her in the face. Why? How had she offended these people? She was aware that John's departure had made some people uncomfortable, but she was reaching out, offering her hospitality.

The oven timer beeped and the kitchen was filled with the sweet scent of apples as she opened the oven door and placed the pie on a cooling rack. After staring at the pile of food on the counter, she wrapped the chicken and placed it in the freezer. The previously frozen shrimp went in the fridge. Unstoppable tears streamed along her cheeks and bounced as they hit the countertop. Gasping and choking, she made no attempt to stop—she no longer cared.

Five

Brianna's Revenge

Melanie put the key in the front door, assuming her mother must be out since there were no lights on except for the hall. She felt the need to be quiet. Leaving her bags by the door, she crept into the lounge. She spotted Buddy as he raised his head, surprised that he hadn't run to greet her. Then she saw her mother curled up on the sofa with Buddy nestled in her middle. He didn't move. Melanie panicked and bent down, relieved to hear her mother breathing. She whispered, "Mum, it's me. Melanie."

Katie tried to open her eyes. Swollen from crying, she could barely see her daughter. Was she dreaming? She sat up on her elbows and Buddy jumped down, allowing Melanie to sit on the edge of the sofa. "Mum, what's wrong?"

Katie could only sob, no words came out. Every tear shed and unshed over the past six months could no longer be held back. Melanie hugged her mother and held her tight.

Comforted by her daughter, she found her voice and smiled. "It used to be me comforting you. Why are you here? Isn't the speaking event next week?"

"It is but I took some holiday and came to surprise you. It looks as though it was a good decision. Mum, I've never seen you so upset. Are you ill? Has Dad been upsetting you? Tell me what's going on."

"No, I'm not ill and I haven't heard from your dad since the final papers. I was fired, and my friends are against me. I don't know why!" Her voice began to quiver.

"Let's open a bottle of wine and you can tell me the whole story. I can't imagine you doing anything worthy of getting fired and what friends? Is it Judy?" Melanie walked into the kitchen. "What's all this food for?"

"The dinner party I had planned for tomorrow. At the last minute, they all declined the invitation. Judy and I are fine. She came around earlier this week, the day I was fired. If you're hungry, make yourself a plate of shrimp. It won't keep."

Katie sat back, exhausted. Her throat hurt and her breathing was erratic as she held back tears. Consciously, she took in several deep breaths and closed her eyes to meditate, but her thoughts were too intense. The breathing had calmed her and the tears abated.

Buddy's nose twitched as he looked up at the food. He trotted by Melanie's side as she carried a tray of shrimp, avocado, French bread, plates and glasses, into the lounge. A bottle of white wine, tucked precariously under one arm, was placed beside the tray on the coffee table.

"Ah, this looks good. I don't get this in Peru. Here, Mum, have some. When did you last eat?"

"Breakfast, I guess." Buddy sat alert at her feet. "Not for little dogs. Ah… okay who could resist that face?" Katie held out a shrimp and Buddy gently took it from her fingers. It was gone in a flash.

"Mum, you shouldn't do that. He'll beg throughout the meal."

"No, he's a good dog." Katie patted his head. His eyes watched every movement. If a shrimp might just drop to the floor, he was ready to pounce.

Melanie poured two large glasses of wine, held up her glass and said, "to better days."

Katie repeated, "Better days." The wine cooled and relaxed her throat. "Tell me about Peru. You look tanned, and the sun bleached your hair. It's a lovely golden brown and its long. Are you happy?"

"Very! I love my work. I love Peru and the people are wonderful."

"It does my heart good to see you so happy. What's the presentation at the university about?"

"The effects that different species of trees have on wildlife and, sadly the lack of trees. Many of the world's forests are disappearing. Trees gobble up bad air and give us good air. Without trees, all animals suffer, including humans. My team is examining samples of bark, roots and leaves for microbes and testing the air surrounding the forest. We have some shocking results and that's what my talk is about."

"What did I do to deserve such a brilliant daughter? Gosh, your work sounds so interesting. I am so boring. You must have your father's brain."

"No Mum, Dad has a pea-brain. My brain is from you. I learned about science and botany from university, but what you showed me, how to love and care for people, can't be taught in schools."

"You're just saying that to make me feel better…and it does. I'm very proud of you. Have you talked to your dad?"

"I have not! Nor, do I want to. I went to see him before I left for Peru and his current girlfriend was celebrating her thirtieth birthday. Two years younger than me! It was pathetic. I walked out."

"It must be hard to see your father like that. He wasn't always so self-absorbed." Seeing Melanie's taut face, she changed the subject. "What's Ben up to? I get brief emails and an occasional text but he doesn't say much."

"He's touring the Americas. Last text I had, he was waiting tables somewhere in Texas, learning to ride, cowboy style." Melanie laughed hard. "I'd love to see that. I doubt he'll ever settle down. Dad hurt him very badly."

Katie nodded in agreement. "Do you think he's all right? I worry about him."

"Stop worrying. He's fine. He works when he needs money and travels when he has money. I keep in touch, even in the wilds of Peru. Thanks to satellites, I can get text messages."

Katie yawned. "The wine is making me sleepy. It has been quite a day. Actually, quite a week."

"Are you going to tell me what happened?" Melanie frowned with a questioning look.

"Can it wait until morning? I'm exhausted."

"Of course. We'll do something nice tomorrow and have a casual chat. I'll stay up for a while since I have work to finish."

"Your bed is made, as always. Clean towels are in the linen cupboard. Can you let Buddy out before you go to bed?" Katie bent down and kissed her daughter. "It's lovely to have you home."

The chilly morning air made Katie pull her housecoat closer as she crept downstairs so as not to wake Melanie. She skimmed the headlines on the Saturday newspaper, placing it on the kitchen table and made coffee. Buddy gave her the look to go out and she opened the back door. A crisp morning greeted them but there was no frost on the lawn today. She stood at the door, listening to the birds chattering a quiet winter morning chorus.

Although she had slept well, she still felt exhausted from the night before. It scared her. Recalling what she might have done, she remembered lying on the sofa thinking of ways to end her life. It was Buddy who snapped her out of such dark thoughts; stroking his back and wondering who would take care of him if she wasn't around. And, now with Melanie here and Ben somewhere in America, Katie knew that, in their own way, they needed her as much as she needed them. She wanted to live and enjoy life.

She shivered as she closed the door and turned the thermostat up. The coffee pot gurgled, ready for the first cup of the day. She sat at the kitchen table, tucking her feet under her and spreading the newspaper out flat to read.

"Good morning, Mum!" Melanie kissed Katie and stretched. "I always sleep so well in my own bed."

"Good morning, dear. Coffee's made. What would you like for breakfast?"

"Coffee's fine for now. I'll go for a run this morning. I need the exercise after the long flight. I'll have breakfast later."

"I'll make us a late breakfast then. Do you have any plans?"

"None. What shall we do today?"

"I'd like to go to Springsville. Take Buddy for a walk along the towpath and have tea at Mary's Café & Bakery. The narrowboats are all moored for the winter but it's still nice out there."

"Perfect. I'm off but I'll be back in half an hour."

Katie relaxed and let Melanie drive the rental car, a nice new Vauxhall with bells and whistles. Buddy, pleased to be sitting on Katie's knee, didn't whine.

"I met Phil when I was leaving for my run this morning and we jogged together. He's a great guy. I've never understood why he isn't married. I wondered if he was gay but he seems quite heterosexual," Melanie added.

"I know what you mean and he is a nice guy but I wonder if there's a mystery somewhere. Other than his work at the university, he doesn't talk about himself at all." Katie gave a gasp and put her hands to her lips. "Oh no, I forgot to tell Phil the dinner party's cancelled tonight!"

"I told him. He chattered a lot this morning. He's fond of you."

"Phil has been kind since your father left. A true friend, which is more than I can say for the other neighbours. Brianna played nice and even got me the job at Becket's, but then turned into a witch."

"Phil had some interesting things to say. He told me what happened at Becket's and he told me about Brianna. I don't wonder you were so upset. You should report Graham Becket to the Ministry of Works and Brianna is just plain nasty." Melanie glanced at her mother.

Katie frowned. "What? Why are you looking at me that way?"

"I have something to tell you. Phil was going talk to you

about this but I said I would tell you. Please don't get upset."

"Melanie! Tell me what?"

"The reason your neighbours turned down dinner was because Brianna has spread a rumour that you were having an affair with Graham Becket."

"That's ridiculous! I hardly know the man. I accused him of sexual harassment. That's why he fired me. Where did Phil hear this silly rumour?"

"Dave told him. Dave didn't believe the rumour, but Anne did."

"That explains why they accepted at first and cancelled later," Katie said.

"Dave has a business connection with Becket Marketing. Hearing the rumours, he asked questions. Brianna started the rumour right after you were fired because Mrs. Becket had uncovered her husband's affair. Not the first time, but she didn't know the name of the woman. You were a convenient scapegoat for both Brianna and Becket."

"But why would she spread a lie to our neighbours? They have nothing to do with Becket."

"Revenge. By suggesting you were the other woman, Brianna thought she could continue the affair. After his wife threatened divorce, Becket broke up with her. His marriage and kids turned out to be more important than Brianna. She assumed you told his wife."

"I don't even know his wife but I can empathize with the poor woman, being married to that brute." Katie was trying hard to swallow tears. The injustice of such accusations was eating at her insides. She brushed a stray tear, willing the others to stay put.

Melanie touched her hand and Katie almost lost it again but

managed a smile. "I'm so grateful you are here."

"I am too. I'll give that woman, and your friends, a piece of my mind. Phil says Brianna has a reputation for gossip."

Buddy stood up with his paws on the car door, his tail wagging frantically as they drove down Marina Lane. Katie almost twisted her neck as she tried to read the estate agents sign perched on the gate post of Lavender Cottage. A strange sense of excitement made her smile. Buddy gave a woof. Katie stroked his head and whispered, "Are you excited too, Bud?"

Melanie swung the car into the parking lot, glancing at her mother. "Why the smile? Not that I'm complaining. It's good to see you smile."

"Nothing. Just nice thoughts, for a change. The Wellington boots are in the back. It gets wet and muddy on the towpath."

"Good thinking, Mum. Come on, let's walk and work off the hurt and anger."

Katie usually walked, sorting out problems, but today she talked, or at least listened, as Melanie rambled on about life in Peru. The towpath was quiet. Perhaps the heavy November cloud promising rain kept everyone at home.

By the time they returned to the car, it was getting cool and looked like rain. Katie left Buddy in the car instead of the Dog Moorings and walked to the café.

"I am ready for a hot cup of tea and hungry for hot buttered scones with strawberry jam. Mary, not only makes the scones, but she makes the jam too," Katie said.

They sat at a window table overlooking the canal basin and narrowboats. Mr. Tranquil Days was walking along the boardwalk from his boat, Arthur yapping at his heels, attracting Katie's attention. His eyes caught hers and he waved. She smiled and waved back.

"Who's that handsome guy?" Melanie asked, with a smile.

"I don't know his name. He owns that narrowboat, *Tranquil Days,*and we had a conversation last time I was here with Judy. Buddy took a fancy to his little dog, Arthur. It's amazing the people you meet when you have a dog."

"You're looking better. How are you feeling?" Melanie said.

"All things considered, good. Angry and frustrated because the whole thing is so unjust but I'll get over it. I never asked how long you're staying?" Katie sat still, waiting for Melanie's answer.

"Ten days all together. I have to go to Nottingham on Monday to meet the Dean of Science and attend some meetings. I'll stay in a hotel until after the talk on Tuesday. Remember, I work for Nottingham University and they are funding this project, so I have to do my due diligence. I'll come home on Wednesday morning and you will have my undivided attention until I leave for Peru on Monday.

"Did you change your plans for me?"

"A little, but I'd rather sleep in my own bed and be with you than talk shop with boring professors."

"Thank you." Katie grinned and hugged her daughter.

Six

Impulsive Moves

*I*t was dusk as they turned into Autumn Road. Katie
pointed to the car in front of them and shuddered.
"That's Brianna's car."

"Mum, don't let her get to you."

"She's spoiled a lovely day."

"I'll fix that." Melanie turned the car in to the driveway
switched the engine off before jumping out of the car and
running across the street. "Brianna, I'd like a word!"

Brianna's keys dropped on the porch as she spun around
and glared at Melanie. "I have nothing to say to you."

"Oh yes, you do. You don't spread gossip like that about my
mother and get away with it."

"What are you talking about? Perhaps there's a side of your
mother you don't know about."

Melanie had a strong urge to slap this woman but held her
hands tight at her sides. Out of the corner of her eye, she could

see her mother crossing the road. Melanie motioned to Katie not to come any further. Her eyes on Brianna, she said, "let's continue the conversation inside—unless you'd like the whole neighbourhood to hear what I have to say?"

"Oh, come in then." Brianna saw Anne and Dave coming out of their front door and gave a wave.

Katie stood at the curb, dumbfounded and stared as her daughter went into Brianna's house. The chilly night air made her shiver. Stepping inside her own house, she watched from the lounge window. Twenty minutes later, Brianna's front door opened and Melanie stepped out, said something, and left. Brianna slammed the door so hard, Katie's windows rattled.

"Mum! Where are you?" Melanie shouted as she entered the house.

"In the lounge."

"Brianna will not bother you again. If she sticks to her side of the bargain, she will set the record straight with your friends."

"What did you say to her?"

"I threatened her with a lawsuit; defamation of character. Brianna is many things, but she's not stupid and is fully aware that she would lose in court. The publicity, which I exaggerated, would ruin her and Graham Becket." Melanie gave a long sigh. "Phew, that was intense! I need a glass of wine."

"Sit. I'll get the wine. I can't tell you how grateful I am. I would never have been able to do what you did." Katie skipped into the kitchen. Brianna would set the record straight and her friends would be back although she wasn't sure she wanted them back. She'd lived on Autumn Road for thirty years. Suburbia had been good when the kids were growing up, a great place for a couple to raise a family. Melanie was two when they moved in and Ben was born here but with no kids or husband, she didn't really belong there anymore.

"Hey Mum, are you brewing the wine from scratch?" Melanie laughed.

"Coming! I was miles away, weighing up why I need to live here. Perhaps I need to move."

"Where would you live?"

"I love Springsville. The last time Judy and I were at Mary's, I said I could live there and Judy said, 'why don't you?.'"

"And?"

"It seemed a silly idea but the same feelings of peace and contentment came over me today."

"I saw you looking at the For-Sale sign. It's a pretty cottage, but it looks run down. Are you considering this because of the problems? I guess what I'm trying to say is, are you running away from Brianna?"

"No, I'm not. It feels like home, a different home to here. It's as though my time on Autumn Road has ended and it's time to move forward. When I saw the For-Sale sign, I was excited."

"Why don't we call the estate agent and make an appointment for tomorrow?"

"Really? Do you think it's a good idea too?"

"Those were not my exact words but I'm warming up to the idea. We need to discuss the pros and cons. This is a big decision." Katie was no longer paying attention; her mind had already moved to Springsville.

The sign on the estate agent's office door read, 'Closed on Sunday' with a phone number. Melanie called from her mobile, left a message and drove to Marina Lane. The aroma of coffee and fresh baked muffins wafted in the air as they walked to Mary's, waiting for the agent to call.

"Hello, again." Mary's friendly voice greeted them as they entered. "What will it be today? Hot muffins just came out of the oven."

"Two coffees and two muffins, please." Katie said, adding, "Do you know anything about the cottage that's for sale?"

"Lavender Cottage?" Mary pointed over her shoulder. "Yes, old Adam Cummings owns it. He moved to his son's place after his wife, Doris, died. It's been empty for about six months and needs work but it's a lovely place. Are you interested?"

Katie nodded. "Yes, I'm just waiting for the estate agent to return our call. I love Springsville and I want to move here." Katie realized how positive she sounded and grinned. "My name is Katie Saunders, and this is my daughter, Melanie."

"Pleased to meet both of you. I'm Mary Bingham. I own the café and bakery and my husband, Bob, owns the marina. Bob and I have lived here for twenty years and love it. Bob was in the navy and needs to be near boats and water and I love to cook. We found our heaven here." She reached a long arm over the counter. Mary was exceptionally tall and slender with a pretty, delicately featured face, framed by short curly grey hair. Katie always imagined a baker to be short and plump. They shook hands.

"I have the key to Lavender Cottage. It saves Janet running over every time someone wants to see it. When she calls, just tell her you're here and she'll call me to give you the key. Coffee's on me."

Half an hour later, Katie pushed open the garden gate and walked down the path as a sweet fragrance filled her nostrils. Lavender bushes lined the walkway; the flowers faded and brown even as the scent lingered. The garden needed work, as did the outside of the cottage. Nothing that hard work and a good paint job wouldn't fix.

The sturdy wooden door creaked as it opened into a large parlour with a massive fireplace and large oak beams overhead. A warm cozy atmosphere filled the room, despite the chill in the air. Melanie had wandered into another large room next to the kitchen, a morning room with a small round table with two chairs. At each side of the fireplace stood two big overstuffed comfy chairs. French doors opened into a rose garden. Katie felt as though she was wrapped in love. The kitchen was surprisingly modern with white cupboards, a dishwasher, fridge and cooker. A large eating area with sliding doors led to a back porch with two rocking chairs. Katie imagined the old couple rocking away with morning coffee or afternoon tea.

The upstairs had three bedrooms and bathroom plus a self-contained suite of two rooms with an en-suite bathroom over the kitchen, obviously an extension built recently. "I wonder why this was built? A granny flat?"

"Could be, or maybe for home care of some sort. Mary said his wife had died so we can assume she'd been ill. This is a big house. What would you do with all these rooms?"

"It is big, but I love the place. Lots of room for you and Ben when you come to visit. I could rent out the suite for extra money." Katie picked up an information sheet and looked at the price. "That's a lot of money."

"Mum, that's an excellent price for the size of the cottage right next to the marina. Do you know the value of your house?"

"The house was appraised for the divorce settlement and it's worth £400,000 so I'd have money left."

"If you sell, will you have to give Dad any money?"

"No, he signed the house over to me." Katie paused and laughed. "It eased his guilty conscience when he spent all our savings on that stupid loft. My solicitor insisted on adding a clause allowing me to sell, rent or do whatever I wanted with the house. At the time, I couldn't imagine doing any of those things but now I'm grateful. I've decided to buy Lavender Cottage." As Katie said the words, a wave of excitement trickled through to her toes.

Melanie's eyebrows pinched together, a habit she'd had since childhood, which meant she was solving a problem.

"I know that look. You are analyzing the situation."

Melanie gave a nod. "Financially, it's a practical choice, but it's a hasty decision. You need to give it some serious thought. It's quite isolated here. You've been used to the mall down the road, doctor around the corner. What happens when you need a job? It's a long commute to either Derby or Nottingham."

"Everyone in the village looks well fed and healthy, I'm sure they manage. Your dad agreed to pay alimony for three years. It's enough to get by and in that time, I can figure out what to do. I'll take online courses, work from home. The one thing I got out of Becket Marketing was learning to use a computer."

"Let's talk about this over lunch. We have to take the key back to Mary's anyway," Melanie said, her eyebrows pinched together as she glanced at her mother.

Katie strolled up to the counter and handed the key to Mary. She whispered, "I love the place and want to buy it. Would you call Janet and ask her to meet me? I want to make an offer." Katie glanced over her shoulder. "Melanie's worried I'm rushing it."

51

Mary smiled and whispered, "Got ya'. I'll call her now." Raising her voice, she said, "so that will be two chicken specials, two coffees and orange cake. Good choice."

Katie ambled back to their table, deciding what to say to her daughter.

"Melanie, I understand your concern and I love you for that, but I have made up my mind. I am buying Lavender Cottage." Melanie interrupted and Katie raised her hand. "I've asked Mary to call Janet to meet us so I can make an offer." Katie put her arm around her daughter and kissed her cheek, squeezing her shoulders. "I want this. It will work out fine."

"Mum, you've never done anything this impulsive. There are a million reason you shouldn't do this. There are so many unanswered questions!"

"I know the scientist needs to analyze. I am being impulsive but it's right for me. So please, be happy for me. I will need your help with the negotiating process. Can you do that for me?"

"Okay! If you insist." Melanie tried a weak smile, but it didn't break the frown.

Janet arrived an hour later and the offer was made on the condition that Katie's house sold. No one doubted that it would sell quickly.

Monday morning, Katie picked up the phone and called Judy.

"Guess what? I bought Lavender Cottage in Springsville."

"Congratulations! I am so happy for you, Katie. You deserve this. Now, tell me what happened. Was Lavender Cottage for sale when we were there?"

"No, Melanie and I went on Saturday and I spotted the sign and bought it on Sunday. Melanie says I'm crazy but I have never been more sane."

"The place is perfect. What condition is the cottage in? I can check it out and make sure the structure is sound."

"Would you? That would be great and it would ease Melanie's concerns. Can we meet at the café on Saturday? You'd get to see Melanie before she goes back to Peru. We could have lunch and inspect the cottage. Mary has the key at the café."

"That would work out fine. Shall I bring the dogs? Lily's paw is better and we could go for a walk."

"Yes. Buddy loves his walks on the towpath. Now there's someone who will like the move—daily walks by the canal." Hearing his name, Buddy sat at Katie's feet and looked up at her, expectantly. She patted his head.

"Do you need an estate agent? I can recommend Gothridge and Sons. I don't know their number offhand but I can email. Katie, I am thrilled; this is a whole new life and you deserve it."

"Thanks Judy, I need your support. I couldn't ask for a better friend. See you Saturday."

Gothridge and Sons came out to see Katie's house that day and the For Sale sign was ordered to go up the next day. Things were moving fast and doubts were creeping into Katie's thoughts. She hadn't told Phil, which was odd as she valued his opinion. The neighbours would make assumptions; right or wrong, she no longer cared.

The afternoon was spent doing things that the estate agent suggested would make the house more appealing to buyers. Reluctantly, Katie removed her knick-knacks. She loved little things, ornaments, memorabilia of trips or kids' milestones, china figurines—they used to drive John crazy. Now she imagined them in the cottage, lots of windowsills and mantelpieces to decorate.

"Knock, knock!"

"Phil, come in. Can I offer you tea, coffee or a glass of wine? I'm celebrating."

"Wine sounds good. Red if you have it, please."

"I have lots of wine, no dinner party. Remember?"

"Ah, yes," Phil paused. "I bumped into Melanie and she told me how upset you were. I wished you'd called me. I'm a good listener."

"Thank you for caring. I was in a bad place and needed to cry."

"Brianna apologized to Anne and Dave, saying the rumour was a mistake. I filled them in with the details. Anne will apologize to you."

"Melanie gave Brianna a piece of her mind. Scared her with threats of lawsuits."

"Ah, that explains it. Melanie is an amazing person. You are lucky to have a family. I'm sorry you've had such a bad time though. You deserve better. What are you celebrating?"

"I am selling the house and I have bought a cottage in Springsville."

"Oh… That was fast."

"Melanie is worried I'm moving too fast. But it's exactly what I want. I wanted you to know before the For-Sale sign goes up tomorrow."

"I agree with Melanie. Are you sure about this?"

"Don't you start? Yes, I am positive! Now let's drink to new beginnings."

"I shall miss you." Phil said, "Gosh, you're the only person on the street, except Dave, that I can call a friend."

"The cottage is large. You can come and visit any time. In fact, we are going on Saturday. Judy has offered to inspect the property to make sure it's structurally sound. Why don't you come along with us?"

"I'd like that, thank you. Will Melanie be coming or has she gone back?"

"No, she's in Nottingham for a couple days. Her talk at the university is tomorrow. She'll be back here Wednesday and flies back to Peru on Monday."

Seven

Melanie's Visit

The sun warmed Katie's face and her insides felt sunny too. Being in Springsville filled her with a sense of anticipation and excitement, something like Santa on Christmas Eve. She parted her lips in a grin.

She waved to Judy on the towpath. Lily and Sammy strained on their leashes as Buddy ran towards them.

"What a fabulous day. Sunshine in November; perfect for a walk," Katie said as she gave Judy a hug.

"I have to say it. I haven't seen you this radiant since Ben's birth. I hope the cottage is sound and you're not disappointed." Judy pulled Sammy away from the water. "No, Sammy, away from the water. He hates being on the leash but the smell of canal water on top of the wet-dog odour is more than I can handle in the car." Judy chuckled. "Do you mind if we walk through the fields before Sammy pulls my arm off?"

Katie nodded agreement, and they climbed over the stile

into the meadow. The thick hawthorn hedge hid the water and Sammy, happy to be off the leash, ran across the field with Lily close behind. Buddy's little legs and chunky body were trying to catch up. "Not a chance, Bud!" Katie laughed.

"Lily will turn around in a minute and join Buddy. Sammy won't be back until he's reached the end of the field." Judy said.

"Judy, do you think there might be problems with the cottage?"

"Old houses can have issues, especially if it's been neglected, but we can fix most things."

"It's good to share my worries with a friend. You're right it might need work. Melanie means well, but she's not convinced I'm doing the right thing and even Phil is being careful of what he says."

"Maybe seeing the place will convince them. The important thing is that it's what you want."

"It is. I'm certain."

"Then it's right for you. You are behaving out of character, the usually quiet, cautious and…"

"Boring and mousy," Katie added

"Well, I wouldn't put it quite like that… Your words, not mine. And, yes, people are seeing a different Katie. People don't like change. They'll get used to it and Melanie is only looking out for you. Why didn't Melanie come with us?"

"She wanted to walk around the canal basin. Phil is familiar with the canal system and the history of narrowboats, so Professor Phil Williams elected to give her a lecture. Peru has nothing like this. She wants to take pictures to show how different it is here to the local Peruvians on her team." Katie glanced at her watch. "We'd better head back. I told them to meet us at the cottage at noon. Melanie was picking up the key."

Phil and Melanie were walking around the garden when they arrived. "It's a lovely garden," Phil said, "and until recently, it has been looked after. Clean-up will be easy in the spring."

"That's good to know. I'm not much of a gardener. I'll hire someone."

"Are you guys coming?" Melanie called, holding the front door open.

"Just settling the dogs. Good dogs, sit and stay!" They looked cute, sitting in a row by the front door, watching their masters disappear into the cottage.

"Phil, would you come with me?" Judy said, "I might need some muscle to lift things. Katie, you and Melanie take a look around and we'll talk about my findings over lunch."

Katie led the way up the stairs as Phil and Judy headed for the hatch to the crawl space.

"I want this bedroom," Melanie said looking at the rose garden. "Ben can have the one overlooking the lane. I know you'd like the one with the view of the water."

"Are you giving me your seal of approval?"

"Yes. I can't deny how happy this place makes you and I agree it's a lovely cottage. If everything checks out, you have my blessing."

Tears sprang into Katie's eyes. "Thank you," she whispered. "Kitchen next. I can't remember how many cupboards there are."

Phil and Judy crossed them on the stairs. "Looks good so far," Judy said over her shoulder.

"Well, that's reassuring."

"Wow," Melanie stopped in the doorway. "I don't remember this. Not what I expected in a cottage kitchen. I like this room.

It's bright and airy and the sliding door to a porch is perfect."

"Mum, let's sit on the porch." Melanie sat on the steps that led to the garden. "That looks like a vegetable garden. I can see marrows and Brussels sprouts. And I think there are potatoes and tomato plants at the back."

Katie nodded, wondering if the garden would be too much for her. She'd never grown anything. Even her indoor plants didn't thrive too well. She lowered herself into one of the rocking chairs.

As the chair rocked gently, Katie heard a voice. *'I'm Doris'.* Katie looked around. For a second, she held her breath, afraid of the voice. What was she hearing? The voice was gentle and instinct told her she need not worry. Surprised at her own reaction, she accepted the presence of a ghost. *'Adam and I lived here; it is a happy home. Adam misses it but he's better off with our son, Kevin. When you move, please invite Adam to visit so he can rock with me for a while.'* Katie looked over her shoulder, but hearing the rhythmic squeak of the other rocking chair as it rocked by itself, she knew Doris was sitting in it. Afraid to speak aloud, she willed her thoughts to Doris. *'My name is Katie and Melanie is my daughter, a scientist. Doris, I love this cottage. It's filled with happiness and love. I'll make sure Adam comes to visit.'* The rocking increased. *'Thank you. I have to go now. Welcome to Lavender Cottage.'* The chair stopped rocking and Katie glanced at Melanie, wondering if she had heard ghostly Doris. Melanie's scientific mind would not understand dead people talking.

Melanie joined her and Katie asked, "How was your walk around the narrowboats? I bet you learned more about narrowboats and the canal basin than you needed."

"Phil gets passionate about things but I kind of like it.

I've lived in this county all my life but I had no idea how important narrowboats were to the economy. All kinds of goods and commodities were transported along the canals before highways. Now we have trucks and motorways spewing exhaust fumes into the environment."

"The environment is important to both you and Phil."

Melanie's cheeks blushed slightly. "Yes. He's almost as passionate about the environment as me."

Katie smiled with affection. "Was anyone in the basin?" Katie changed the subject seeing Melanie blush. "It's a quiet time of the year."

"We stopped and chatted to a man about your age. He was taking his boat out. He told us he came every weekend from Nottingham and offered us a ride, but we didn't have time. Nice man. He had a little dog called Arthur. When I mentioned Buddy, he said Arthur and Buddy were friends. Who is he?"

"Mr. *Tranquil Days*. I don't know his name. The dogs kind of introduced themselves a couple of weeks ago."

"I like it here. Next time I come to visit, at Christmas, will you have moved in?" Melanie glanced at her mother.

"I'd like to be but it depends on the sale of Autumn Road."

"All done!" Judy said, leaning out of the kitchen door. "I'm hungry." The four walked to the café.

"Structurally, the cottage is sound. The roof and foundation are in excellent condition. It needs a paint job, caulking around the windows but the structure is sturdier than many new buildings. There's a garage at the back, used for storage. The wood is rotten in places and it will need repairing but it doesn't affect the cottage. The garden needs tidying but, Katie, it's a good buy. I suggest you firm up the offer as soon as you can."

"I can help with the garden," Phil said. "I like the natural layout. It must be the environmentalist in me. Melanie had some interesting things to say about the natural growing patterns of trees and plants in her talk at the university."

"I didn't realize you went to Melanie's talk. Makes me prouder than I already am. Tell me about her speech?" Katie glanced at Melanie's cheeks, which had turned pink. She smiled wondering if Melanie being modest, which would be unusual, or was romance in the air?

"Melanie is amazing. She's knowledgeable, funny and very personable. She is an excellent speaker. I was mesmerized for two hours." Phil grinned.

After lunch, Melanie and Phil went to the car while Judy and Katie retrieved the dogs from Dog Moorings.

"Is it my imagination, or is there something going on between my daughter and Phil?" Katie asked.

"I saw it too." Judy nodded her agreement. "They make a nice pair."

"Isn't he a bit old for Melanie?" Katie frowned

Judy rolled her eyes. "Really, Katie! Do a few years matter?"

"You're right. No, it doesn't matter. We're speculating and Melanie leaves for Peru tomorrow."

The car door closing and the engine starting sounded loud in the early morning quiet. Katie struggled to keep her emotions in tact as Melanie drove off to the airport. She reflected on the past week. Ten days ago, she'd lain on the sofa, so despondent she wanted to end it all. Melanie had arrived at the right time. Now, life was changing so fast she wanted to put the brakes on. She blew a kiss as the red rear lights disappeared around the corner. Having Melanie home had made everything easy."Suck it up! You promised your daughter you would manage. Time to pull up the big girl panties," she added aloud, wrapping her arms around her middle and shivering. Seeing the frost glisten on the front lawn, she wished she'd worn her coat.

Buddy sat, waiting for his walk. "Not yet Bud. It's 4:30 a.m. Garden for you. We'll go for a walk later." Katie opened the back door. Buddy ran out and Katie debated between hot coffee or returning to bed. She decided on coffee. She could use the time to clean up the house. Gothridge & Sons texted that the young couple who had seen the house yesterday wanted a second viewing at lunchtime.

The house shone by the time Katie finished cleaning and polishing. Exhausted, she would have liked to nap, but the estate agent had booked an appointment for 1 p.m. Katie showered, changed and waited. The wait caused anxiety and doubt crept into her mind *What if I'm making a mistake? I've never made such a big decision*. She almost jumped off her chair when the doorbell rang.

A tall young man, in his late twenties, stood on the doorstep. He was dressed in a business suit with his arm around a pretty, pregnant woman. A little voice said, "Hello." Katie's eyes found a cute little boy, two or three years old, looking up at her.

"Hello, young man. What is your name?"

"Kyle. We've come to see your house. We came yesterday too."

Katie smiled and replied, "Pleased to meet you Kyle."

"Rodney West," the young man said. "This is my wife, Maddy, and our son, Kyle, who you already met." Rodney grinned. "We've been teaching him not to be shy when meeting new people."

"He's doing a great job." Katie offered her hand. "I'm Katie

Saunders. Please come in and wander around. If you have questions, I'll be in the lounge."

Katie sat on the sofa, taking a deep breath. Déjà vu. Rodney and Maddy were John and Katie, thirty years ago. Unexpected sadness sprang into her eyes as she remembered how happy they had been the day they bought this house. It was brand new then.

"Mrs. Saunders?" Rodney's voice came from the hall. "Could we ask you some questions?"

"Of course. What would you like to know?"

"Do you mind if I ask you why you are moving?"

"Not at all. When John and I moved here, I was pregnant with Ben and Melanie was two years old, a family just like yours, and suburban life was perfect for us. Our children are adults and have flown the nest now. We are looking for a quieter life in the country." Katie noted that she'd said we and not *I*, she didn't want this couple to know their happy life had ended in divorce. "Springsville, a cottage by the marina to be exact."

"That brings me to my next question. When can we take procession? We gave notice to our landlord and have to be out of the flat by December 1st and we'd like to settle in before the baby is born. We had a deal, but it was in a chain and one sale fell through at the last minute."

"That must have been disappointing. I've already bought the cottage, my new place, and there's no chain of buyers. The cottage is empty so I can move anytime. December 1st would be perfect. When is the baby due?"

Maddy answered, "January 15th, so it only gives us a six weeks. I'm glad the other deal fell through. I like this house much better. It's a loving, caring home."

"Sometimes things work out for the best. This has been a wonderful home. I shall miss it, but knowing a family like yours is taking over, makes it easier to leave."

Rodney took Maddy's hand in his and put his arm around Kyle. "We'll call the estate agent and make you an offer this afternoon. Excuse me for rushing but I have to get back to work."

When Katie closed the front door, her feet wanted to do a jig of happiness. Selling the house to Rodney and Maddy was like passing the baton to the next generation. She liked them. They would take care of the house and once again 23 Autumn Road would be a family home, filled with love and laughter.

Eight

Lavender Cottage

⟐

The empty moving truck pulled away after unloading Katie's belongings and tucking them into Lavender Cottage. She strolled down her garden path, brushing her fingers against the lavender bushes. She couldn't help but pinch her arm. In less than two months she had divorced, found a job, gotten fired, fallen into the depths of despair and risen to blissful happiness. She had sold her house and bought a cottage in Springsville.

Katie surveyed the parlour and found a corner of the sofa to sit on, wondering where to start. Her tummy rumbled with hunger and she realized it was getting dark and she hadn't eaten since a coffee and a muffin at ten that morning. Grabbing her purse and coat, she looked around for Buddy but remembered Buddy was at Judy's house for a few days because the packing was making him agitated. She locked the front door and walked to Mary's café.

"How's the move going?" Mary called over the counter.

"I'm all moved in but what a mess. It'll take me forever to get organized and I forgot to eat."

"What do you fancy? The selection is slim. I close at four in the winter. I can make you a sandwich with salad."

"Oh Mary, I didn't realize." Katie glanced at her watch it was 5:10 p.m. "I can go across to the pub."

"No, just turn the closed sign for me, so folks don't think I'm still open and I'll make you a sandwich. You can eat while I clean up and then I'll join you for a cup of tea. I hope you don't mind tea? The coffee machines are all cleaned for the morning."

"Tea is perfect."

"Ham and cheese okay?"

"Perfect too."

The café door rattled. "Katie would you mind letting my husband in."

Bob frowned and stared over Katie's head. "Why d'you lock the door?"

"Bob, this is Katie. She just moved in next door. I'm making her a sandwich."

"Hello Bob," Katie said, "Sorry, it was me. I locked the door when Mary asked me to turn the closed sign."

Bob gave a raspy laugh. "City folk. We don't lock our doors except maybe at night." His voice softened as he added, "Welcome to Springsville Katie. You made a good choice buying Adam's place. We live at Marine Cottage next to you."

Bob walked around the counter, wrapping his arms around Mary's waist kissing her cheek. "How's your day been, sweetie? Need any help?"

"A good day and I'm all done but thanks for offering. You

have a smoke while I have a visit with our new neighbour."

"Okay, I'll go check the moorings while I'm at it." Bob nodded to Katie and left.

Mary came from behind the counter, a mug of tea in each hand and a plate balanced on her arm. "I made us a mug instead of little cups. I figured you needed it and I definitely do. Eat up, you look starved."

"This looks yummy, thank you. I am hungry. Bob's not joining us?"

"Bob's gone to have a smoke. He loves his pipe, but the smoke makes me cough so he always goes outside. Tell me about yourself. Is there a Mr. Saunders?"

"Ran off with another woman. Mid-life crisis." Katie rolled her eyes. "We're divorced. Two children, Melanie you've met and Ben, my baby." She giggled. "Ben turned thirty-one this year but he'll always be my baby. I tired of suburbia, fell in love with Springsville, and here I am."

"I thought you had a story. You were here one day with your friend with the golden retrievers and you looked so sad."

"I had a difficult time. I thought we were a happy couple. Anyway, it's in the past now. New beginnings." Katie relaxed. Talking to Mary was so easy. She'd found a new friend and before she realized it, she'd told Mary her life story.

"I'm doing all the talking. How long have you lived here?"

"Twenty years but the locals only accepted us in the last ten. Don't expect a welcome from the old timers for ten years." Mary grinned. "I come from Barrow-on-Trent, a little village near to here. Bob and I were grammar school sweethearts, but when he joined the navy, we lost touch. I worked in Nottingham selling domestic appliances."

"So how did you and Bob meet again? This sounds romantic."

"It was romantic but not at first. When we had a new line of cooking stoves in the shop, I used to give cooking demonstrations in a display kitchen. I was showing the audience how to bake savoury scones and Bob stopped to watch, and then waited until I'd finished. I recognized him right away. He had not changed, still handsome and tanned—he'd put on a few pounds and lost some hair." She laughed. "I presumed if he was buying appliances, he was married. I thought it inappropriate for him to be flirting with me so, I gave him the brush off."

"Was he married?"

"No. After his navy discharge, he'd rented a flat and come to buy a toaster and kettle. But I didn't know that. Remember it's been twenty years since we left school."

"So, what happened?"

"Bob wouldn't give up. He kept popping into the shop. I became angry, assuming there was a wife. After about three weeks, he asked my colleague if I was married and she told him 'no.' He walked right up and said, 'why don't you like me anymore?' I replied 'because you're married.' He laughed his head off and told me he thought I was married. And the rest is history. We married a month later."

"How did you finish up here?"

"We married late in life. We didn't have kids or schooling to worry about and neither of us liked city living. Bob had a nice nest egg and severance pay. I hated my job and Bob hated the confines of our little flat. He needed to be near water. So we drove out here one day to find the café closed and up for sale. We bought it. The owner of the marina hired Bob to manage the place and when the old man died, Bob bought the marina."

The bell on the café door jingled as the door opened and

Bob walked in. "You two still yakking. Where's my tea? I'm hungry."

"Sorry," Katie said. "I must unpack and let you enjoy your evening." Katie felt embarrassed taking up so much of Mary's time.

"Oh, just a minute." Mary said, "I put a few bits in a bag for you. Just milk, tea and a couple of muffins for your breakfast."

"Thank you, that's very kind. Good night!"

Walking back to Lavender Cottage Katie thought about Bob; how he came across gruff and grumpy but judging by the way he treated Mary she suspected her had a soft, kinder side to him.

As she turned the key to unlock the front door, she smiled remembering Bob's comment about locked doors or not locking doors that will take some getting used to. She looked down, expecting Buddy to greet her. It was quiet without him and she missed him even though Judy planned to bring him the next day and had offered to spend the weekend helping unpack and organize. Judy's organizational skills were second to none and Katie was bracing herself to be ordered around but it would be worth it.

Katie wandered through to the kitchen and opened a couple of boxes but didn't have the energy to unpack. The pitch-black night disconcerted her until she realized there were no street lights or manmade glow in the sky. The kitchen light lit up the porch and she saw Doris' chair rocking to and fro. Katie pulled her coat around her and sat in the other chair and waited. A gentle breeze wafted over her and she heard Doris whisper. *'I see you've moved in. You'll like it here; it's a happy home. Do you remember me talking about Adam?'*

"Yes, but where do I find him?"

'Kevin brings him for breakfast on Sunday morning after church. Sometimes she's with him.'

Katie sensed Doris didn't like her daughter-in-law. "I'll introduce myself and invite Adam over for tea or coffee."

'He likes tea strong, lots of sugar and just a touch of milk. Coffee, lots of milk and one spoon of sugar.'

Katie smiled. "I'll try to remember."

'One more thing. You are very trusting, Katie. Not everyone in this village is as nice as they seem. Be careful...' Doris' voice faded and before Katie could respond, the chair stopped rocking and the air went still.

Katie rocked, feeling content and confident she had made the right decision moving to Springsville. Mary's kindness had sealed the deal so to speak but what did Doris mean by 'Not everyone in this village is as nice as they seem'? She gave an involuntary shiver, sensing something sinister. "Katie, it's December 1st. It's supposed to be cold outside. There's nothing sinister in a cool evening." Yawning, weary and tired, she climbed the stairs, glad she had made up her bed.

A familiar woof and whine at the front door prompted Katie to run and greet Buddy who jumped into her arms. Lily and Sammy bounded down the path as Judy, loaded with grocery bags she used her foot to close the garden gate.

"I figured we'd need some food to keep our strength up."

"Come in, come in." Katie put Buddy to the floor and took the bags from Judy. The dogs rushed around from room to room. Buddy found his bed by the fireplace. He went around in circles and plonked himself down, claiming his territory. Lily and Sammy lay down by the fireplace—the only place that didn't have boxes.

"We'll start with the kitchen. I'll unpack and you put things away where you want them to go." Judy said pulling a box marked china.

"This cupboard will do." Katie opened the cupboard door.

Judy put her hands on her hips and sighed. "Your dishes would be better by the dishwasher. The pans down there and the mugs near the coffee pot. The casserole and serving dishes..." Judy laughed. "I'm being bossy, right?"

"A bit. This is a small kitchen and we need to make good use of the space. And you're good at that. I think I'll unpack and you can put away."

"Great idea."

The dogs slept with an occasional dreamy woof and Judy and Katie worked until the kitchen was organized.

The rhythmic ding-dong of the church bell calling the faithful woke Katie. Stiff from sleeping soundly, she stretched cat-like before getting out of bed. Sunday morning, she thought. Adam would be at the café, having breakfast after church.

Judy was already sitting at the kitchen table with her first cup of coffee. "Good morning! Coffee's made. I thought we could take the dogs for a walk before we tackle the lounge and dining room. That won't take long."

"I'd like to have breakfast at Mary's café. I'm told the locals go after church on Sunday."

"Okay. We'll do that first and then walk the dogs."

The café was buzzing with boaters, locals and people stopping for breakfast. Katie and Judy found an empty table. Katie

71

scanned the tables. Only having seen Adam once, when they closed the house deal, she wasn't sure she'd recognize him, but then it was early, the church service was still in progress. As one group left, another came in, dressed in their Sunday best. Katie figured they were the churchgoers. She spotted Adam Cummins leaning heavily on a cane, frail and sad. A man she assumed was his son, Kevin, guided him to a table. A glamorous woman stepped forward and aggressively pushed Kevin into a chair. Katie guessed the woman was Kevin's wife and the reason Doris disliked her so intently was obvious.

Katie made eye contact with Adam and waved. He waved back and told his son something before he and Sonia looked over. Kevin smiled and nodded; Sonia only giving a haughty glance.

Katie felt uncomfortable and knew someone was staring at her at the next table. Afraid to turn and look, she tried to see through her peripheral vision. Two men sat at the table, one she didn't know but the other was familiar. Curiosity got the better of her and she turned to see Mr. *Tranquil Days* smiling in her direction.

"Good morning! This is a busy spot on Sunday."

"It is, I'm usually here on Saturday, but my friend, who's from out of town wanted to see my boat. And you?"

"I just moved here, yesterday to be exact. I bought Lavender Cottage. My friend Judy has been helping me unpack. Where's Arthur?" The waitress put two enormous plates of breakfast on their table.

"I left him on the boat. It's a bit too cold to leave him outside today."

"Get him one of those doggie coats. But if he's anything like Buddy, he wouldn't wear it." Katie smiled.

"Never. Arthur in a prissy doggie coat? That won't happen." He gave Katie a cheeky grin. "Nice to see you again."

"More coffee?" the waitress asked, putting two large breakfast plates in front of Katie and Judy.

"No thanks," they said in unison.

Judy gave Katie a grin. "That's the guy you waved to sometime back. I think he likes you."

"Please, Judy. Men could not be further from my mind. I'm sorry I didn't introduce you but I don't know his name. Here, eat up. This looks good."

Katie looked up from her breakfast to see Adam leaning on his cane and catching his breath. "Mrs. Saunders. I see you've moved in."

"Yes, yesterday and please call me Katie." She looked around for a spare chair.

Mr. *Tranquil Days* said, "Here take this chair, we're leaving." He pushed the chair to the table and his smile lingered.

"Thank you," Adam said. "My legs don't hold up too well these days. I miss the cottage and the garden, but I couldn't manage any more. My Doris kept telling me it was too much. When she died, it felt empty. Are you happy in the cottage?"

"I love the cottage. You are welcome to come and visit anytime. The rocking chairs are still on the porch." Katie gave him a smile. "When I sit in the chair by the door, I often have company." She glanced at him knowingly. "Come over and join us."

Adam's eyes, watery and red, opened wide. "She's talked to you?"

"Yes. She misses you."

Adam glanced over his shoulder towards his son. "Please don't say anything to Kevin. He doesn't understand and Sonia gets mad."

"It's our secret. When would you like to come?"

"Is Monday too soon? I'll call you first."

"Monday it is." Katie helped him up and walked him back to his table.

"Kevin, I have invited your father to come and visit Lavender Cottage whenever he wants."

"Thank you. Dad misses the cottage. Perhaps Sonia would give him a drive. She works from home."

"I'm too busy, Kevin. He's your father, you can drive him." Sonia's shrill voice hurt Katie's ears. Something in her tone made her flinch.

"Do you live far? I can pick you up, Adam," Katie said. "I don't work at the moment so it would be no trouble."

"At the old vicarage on the bypass," Adam said. "A ten-minute drive. Thank you and maybe I could get a taxi one way."

"Typical." Sonia squinted and frowned, looking irritated. "You always expect people to run after you." Sonia's response seemed excessive and Adam looked distressed and anxious. Katie understood why Doris worried.

"I must get back to my friend. See you tomorrow, Adam."

Judy had finished breakfast. "What was that all about?"

"Adam misses the place. He and Doris used to rock on the porch and he wants to capture some memories. All is not well in that household. Sonia is a piece of work."

"I can tell, she's got that look of superiority."

"Selfish b.i.t.c.h."

"Oh, she rubbed you the wrong way! Come. Finish your breakfast and let's get the dogs and work off some of those calories," Judy said, getting up from the table.

The cottage felt cool when they returned from their walk.

Judy touched the radiator and noticed the central heating wasn't working. "Katie, there's something wrong. You might need a new boiler or expensive repair. I'm sorry I missed it on the inspection."

"Don't worry about it."

"The stack of wood in the garage and the well-used fireplace in the morning room should have given me a clue. I'll arrange for someone to check it out this week."

"Thank you. Let's light a fire and have a glass of wine before you leave. I can finish the unpacking tomorrow."

Katie took the wheelbarrow that was propped up against the fence and wheeled it to the garage. They filled it to the brim with firewood. Judy, somewhat stronger than Katie, pushed the heavy barrow to the back porch. As they stacked it under the shelter of the porch, Judy spoke. "There, that should keep you going until the boiler is repaired."

Nine

Adam Comes to Visit

Katie liked the cozy morning room after lighting a fire. She stared at the straight back chairs that belonged in the kitchen. "I need new chairs. No, I don't. I'll move the lounge chairs." Katie manhandled the two big easy chairs into the morning room, leaving the lounge looking bare, with just a sofa. She arranged the chairs, one on each side of the fireplace, added two side tables and stepped back to admire her work. "And I haven't even put the coffee on yet."

Buddy whined. "Oh, sorry, Bud, I moved your bed. Here you are, back where it belongs." Buddy did a few circles and settled down, tucking his nose under his tail while Katie made coffee.

Several boxes of unpacked books stood next to the bookcases. She ripped off the tape and began arranging the books before the coffee sputtered to a stop. Poking the fire, she sat down to enjoy her morning coffee and glanced at the stray book in her hand The afghan from the back of the chair was warm on her legs as she settled in for a couple of hours reading. She'd worked hard and deserved a break.

Time slipped away as it often did when she had her head in a book. While in the chaos of the divorce, she had missed reading. Buddy barked at the front door but no one knocked. Katie frowned. "What's wrong Bud?" Buddy's bark was getting ferocious, most unlike him. She opened the front door to find an impatient Sonia tapping her foot.

"Oh, Sonia, I'm sorry. I didn't hear you knock."

"I didn't. I'm waiting for *him*." She whipped her head to the side.

Katie saw Adam struggling down the path. "I thought *you* were coming to pick him up?" A huffing sound came from her throat as she thrust her nose in the air and without waiting for an answer she added. "I have clients today."

"I'm sorry. I lost track of time," Katie said feeling guilty because she had forgotten about Adam but then remembered they had not talked about time.

Sonia waved her arm in a '*whatever*' motion and called over her shoulder, "He's all yours. Call a taxi when you've had enough or Kevin will pick him up on his way home from work."

Katie stared at Sonia. Her attitude shocked her. She hadn't planned on Adam being there so early or for the whole day but it was fine. She took his arm, watching Sonia leap into her car and drive off in a cloud of dust. "I guess she's in a hurry."

"She's always in a hurry." Adam said.

"You're limping today. Did you hurt yourself?"

"I slipped in the bathtub. It's nothing. I need to be more careful."

Buddy had stopped barking. Katie guessed he didn't like Sonia but Adam was okay because Buddy curled up on his bed as soon as Adam lowered himself into the easy chair.

"Ah, this is cozy. I used to light a fire for Doris. The central heating is not great." He looked at Katie with an apologetic grin.

"I noticed yesterday. That's why I started a fire. I'll get the heating checked but this is lovely." She handed him a cup of coffee.

"Thank you." He took a sip. "How did you know how I like my coffee?"

"One sugar and a lot of milk. Doris told me."

"She really did talked to you?"

"Yes. She didn't say much. Just that she missed you and how you loved the garden, how you liked your coffee in the morning and how you preferred a strong tea with a little milk and lots of sugar in the afternoon. She also knows you aren't happy about being at Kevin's but she says you needed looking after."

"Kevin does his best but Sonia doesn't want me there. She's…. Can I go out to the porch?"

"Of course. Go ahead and I'll bring your coffee."

Katie picked up the dark blue afghan and draped it across his legs once he was seated. His coffee fitted on the little table and he seemed content. "I'll come and get you in a little while. It's too cold to stay out long," she said, leaving him to connect with Doris. She heard him talking but didn't intrude. Buddy had followed him out, his ears perking up as his head rolled from side to side, listening to Doris.

Katie climbed the stairs to unpack the linen and changed the guest bed in case anyone came to visit. Gazing idly out of the window, she saw Adam wondering around the garden, pulling the overgrown vegetation. Her heart was sad for the man. He'd parted from everything he loved. "Well, the least I can do is help him enjoy some of his days." By the time Katie was back in the kitchen, the French doors were open and Adam was pruning the roses. The sun had peered out from grey clouds and, surprised at its warmth, she stood at the door watching him. His face was bright, the sadness gone as he concentrated on the roses, chuntering away under his breath.

"Time for lunch. Can I make you a cheese sandwich and chicken noodle soup?"

He looked up from the roses. "I like cheese sandwiches. Did Doris tell you that too?"

"No, it's all I have until I go shopping. Thank you for pruning the roses. I don't know the first thing about gardening."

"I found the secateurs in the garage. I hope you don't mind. I left my tools here since I've no use for them at Kevin's."

"You can come by any time to use your tools. I could do with some help in the garden."

They sat at the kitchen table in silence but it was a pleasant one. After they'd eaten, Adam cleared the table and washed the dishes. He grinned. "Dishes are my job. Doris cooked. She always said I couldn't boil an egg and she was right."

"Are you tired? Would you like me to drive you home?" The fear in his eyes startled her. What was he afraid of? "Or," she added, "you can stay until Kevin picks you up."

"Thank you. If I'm not in the way, I like being here, close to Doris. Married for fifty-eight years and every day I told her I loved her. I never missed a day."

"Stay as long as you like. As long as you don't mind if I get on with unpacking."

Katie moved into the lounge and unpacked her little knick knacks and placed them on the mantelpiece and deep window sills. She even saved some for the bookcases in the morning room. Judy was not the frilly type and would have thrown them in the dustbin if she'd had her way but the little things made a house 'home' for Katie. They also sent her down memory lane: the little flowerpot doll Melanie had made in kindergarten, the wooded box Ben created with his dad for a long-ago Mothering Sunday, the Royal Doulton figurines John had bought for her fortieth birthday. She remembered how thrilled she was because he'd gone to the trouble of finding which one was her favourite even though she suspected Melanie had helped him choose. Happy times and lovely memories, she vowed to hold on to the good memories and move forward. Gentle snores came from the morning room—Adam was sound asleep.

The sun streamed into the west facing lounge and she could see blue sky—a lovely afternoon for a walk by the canal. Buddy jumped up when he saw Katie pull on her Wellington boots. She placed a note on the side table to tell Adam they would be back shortly.

Buddy bounded down the towpath and Katie followed with a spring in her stride too. As they reached the little bridge, she heard the drone of an engine and a bark. A green and gold narrowboat with a red roof dawdled along the canal; it was *Tranquil Days*. She waved more enthusiastically than she'd intended. The boat slowed down and stopped when it reached the bridge.

"Hello! Hop on I'll give you a ride to the marina."

Katie hesitated but Arthur barked and Buddy jumped on board, leaving Katie with little choice. "How do I get on?"

"Jump!" Katie's eyes popped out of her head at the thought of jumping off the bridge. Mr. *Tranquil Days* laughed. "Just teasing. I'll pull into the side." Katie hurried from the bridge and stood on the shore. "Here, grab my hand." He gripped her wrist as securely as she held his. "You're okay. I won't let you fall." His firm hold led her over the gap and safely on board.

She settled on a padded seat as he took the tiller and reversed the engine. With expert precision, he guided the boat under the bridge and along the canal.

"Welcome to *Tranquil Days*. My name is Piers Bannister."

"Kaitlyn Saunders but everyone calls me Katie. Piers is an unusual name. Where does it come from?"

"My ancestors come from Normandy, as does the name Piers. It's a variation of Pierre or Peter and, although not French sounding, Bannister is also from Normandy."

"I can't say much about mine. Saunders is my married name." Piers raised his eyebrows with surprise and Katie hastened to add, "Oh, I'm divorced. My maiden name was Jones. My father's family are Welsh but nobody has lived in Wales for decades."

"How are you liking Springsville?"

"Two days and I haven't been this happy for a while. You don't live in the village?"

"I live in Nottingham but if I could, I would live here."

Katie had a flash of doubt. What was she doing on this man's boat? She knew nothing about him and he could be married or worse, a criminal.

"Excuse me for asking but, are you married?"

Piers grinned, "Why do you ask?" An awkward silence ensued. His grin changed into an incredible expression of pain. He took a sharp breath, forcing a smile. "Here we are.

I'll pull into the moorings and make us some tea. It's a little early for wine."

"I'm sorry but I can't stay. I have a visitor. Adam used to live in Lavender Cottage and misses it. I left him snoozing but he'll be wondering where I am."

"All right. Another time, perhaps?"

Katie nodded, looking up at him as he offered his hand to steady her as she stepped onto the dock. *He has bright blue eyes.* For a second she wondered if she'd spoken aloud. "I must go. Come, Buddy."

Adam was awake and sitting on the porch holding a flip phone when Katie returned. "Kevin just called. He's finishing up at the office and he'll pick me up in about an hour," Adam explained, as he rubbed his leg.

"Is that still hurting? Do you mind if I look?" Katie bent down and rolled his trouser leg up to his knee, revealing the wound. She gasped, shocked at the festering injury. "That is a nasty graze," she said to cover her surprise. Helping Adam inside, she cleaned the wound with Dettol. He flinched, as the Dettol stung the large, raw wound. "I'm sorry but I need to clean it. I'll put ointment on it and cover it with a plaster."

The doorbell rang and Katie called out. "Come in! We're in the morning room."

"Hello." Kevin stopped, glancing at Adam's leg and then at Katie. "Dad, what happened?"

"Oh, it's nothing. I slipped in the bathtub this morning. It was hurting so Katie was kind enough to put a plaster on it."

Katie looked up from her nursing. "It's a nasty wound. If it doesn't get better, I'd have a doctor check it." She was doubtful that it had happened that morning or even on the bathtub. It looked more like a cut or graze. Should she say something?

"There, that should help it heal," Katie said, pressing the edges of the plaster and pulling his trouser leg down over his sock.

Kevin's surprise was genuine, as was his concern. "Dad, you should have told me." He helped Adam out of the chair and handed him his cane. "We need to go. We have to pick up Christina from her grandmother's and Sonia will have dinner ready."

"Beans on toast again." Adam rolled his eyes.

"Dad, don't be like that. She does her best."

Adam shrugged at Kevin, leaned on his cane and gave Katie a peck on the cheek. "It's been a lovely day."

Kevin took his father's arm. "Thank you, Katie. I think Dad had a nice time and I will take him to the doctor."

"That's a good idea. Take care, Adam."

Katie walked to the gate with them and watched them drive off. "I think there'sa story there. Christina must be his granddaughter, but he never mentioned her and neither has Doris. Strange!"

Ten

Katie Meets the Village

*K*atie opened the fridge door. The contents were pathetic. A half pint of milk, half a loaf, and a bottle of red wine. She poured a glass of wine and poked the fire into action. Wine made her hungry, but it also prevented her from driving to ASDA for groceries. It was too late to eat at Mary's but the Boater's Inn did pub meals. *I'll get to know the locals,* she thought, finishing her wine. She put on lipstick and pulled the clip from her hair, letting it fall to her shoulders. Not sure how dog-friendly the pub was, she left Buddy in his bed.

Shoulders hunched against the chilly night air, Katie walked up to Main Street. It was shorter across the village green but she thought safer on the road. Her city logic still prevailed.

Cigarette smoke wafted as she passed the smokers standing by the entrance and loud chatter filled her ears as the door opened. She had expected a quiet night since most pubs were slow on a Monday's, but not the Boater's Inn, it was a busy place. It occurred to her that she had never been in a bar unaccompanied, prompting the urge to run home. Several people nodded and said hello, so she took a deep breath and walked up to the bar.

"You're the new girl, what moved into Adam's place, right? I'm Maisie Talbot, proprietor." Maisie stretched a chubby hand across the bar, squeezing ample bosom that could pop out of her dress at any moment.

Katie took her hand and shook it, finding the wobbling boobs distracting. "Katie Saunders. I moved in on Friday."

"What's your poison, duck?"

Poison? Katie thought and then realized Maisie was asking what she wanted to drink. She smiled at the endearment, 'duck' being Nottingham slang.

"Red wine, please, and do you have a menu?"

"Only Shepherd's Pie, today. Monday's a slow night."

"Shepherd's Pie sounds perfect." Katie paid and carried her wine to a table by the window, trying to look invisible. The newcomer interested the locals so no sooner had she sat down than a tall, portly man, brimming with ego sat across from her.

"Cyril Winthrop," he announced, extending his hand. "I own the Springsville Antique Shop." Katie decided that if he pronounced his words with anymore precision, he'd trip over them. With such a heavy county accent, she wondered which estate he was from. Chatsworth was not far.

"Katie Saunders. I just moved into Lavender Cottage."

"Where did you live before coming here?"

"Autumn Road, in a suburb near Derby."

"Ah, if I recall, its near St. Thomas School for Boys. My son attended that school. A damn good school! It's been there years, long before those little box houses. A damn shame to ruin the countryside with boxes."

"I lived on the north end, the older section. The houses have more character than the new ones." Katie wondered why she was defending herself to this man.

"Can't have as much character as Adam's place. It's a hundred years old."

"It's a different way of life. Do you live in the village?"

Cyril ignored her question and she suspected he liked his own ideas as much as the sound of his own voice. "My specialty is rare antiques. You should come by the shop. You'll need furniture more suited to the house. I bought some rare paintings that would suit Lavender Cottage."

"My furniture is fine, thank you. I have a more traditional taste but I could do with chairs for the lounge."

Maisie placed a hot plate in front of her. Entwined in her fingers were condiments: a bottle of HP Sauce, salt and pepper, and napkins. Katie was impressed that everything had made it to the table in an upright position.

"Now, Cyril, leave her alone." She looked at Katie. "He'd sell his own mother, would this one." She punched him playfully on the arm. "Get back to your beer on the bar and let Katie eat in peace."

The Shepherd's Pie was homemade; she smiled traveling back in time remembering her mother's cooking. Of course, it's Monday. Left over roast from Sunday, ground, and made into either a Shepherd's or Cottage Pie, depending on whether it was beef or lamb. This pie was excellent. She'd no sooner finished her pie when, Maisie brought a dish of treacle pudding, swimming in thick custard.

"Here you are. It's on the house. My Stevie's favourite, and there was some left over from dinner."

"Thank you, but…" Katie was about to say she didn't eat pudding, but one look at Maisie told her it would be a mistake to refuse. "My mum used to make this. It was one of Dad's favourites."

"Most men like it. My Bill liked it, God rest his soul. He died last year; cancer took him and the old bugger left me this place. Stevie helps, but he has his limitations." Maisie looked towards the bar and Katie followed her gaze to a young man in his twenties, short and heavy set with a round baby face. Katie wondered if he had Down Syndrome as he concentrated on pulling pints, his eyes always lowered.

"I'd best get back. Another wine?"

"No, thank you. I've had my share of wine tonight." She watched Maisie's ample hips sway as she walked on her high heels, wisps of dyed red hair escaping the hair clip to hang down her back. *Am I stereotyping?* Maisie was Katie's image of a typical barmaid but she suspected the woman was also bright and clever under the short skirts and low cut tops. She ran the pub well.

Katie left Boater's Inn and walked to the narrowboats along the boardwalk, digesting the excellent dinner. Beams of moonlight reflected off the polished brass fittings on the boats. *Tranquil Days* seemed to shine more than the others. The moon, a bright silver disk, was mirrored in the calm water and reminded her of Piers. She'd glimpsed a reflection of a different man and she suspected something terrible had happened in his past. Piers spent a lot of time at the marina, often on weekdays when most people were working. She wondered what he did for a living. Her nose twitched smelling pipe tobacco she turned looking for Bob. A wisp of smoke swirled in the moonlight from the side of a boat.

"Good evening Bob!" she called.

Bob looked up and waved. "A gorgeous night for a walk. But there's a storm blowing in tomorrow. I'm checking the moorings."

"How does the saying go? There's a calm before the storm."

"Something like that. After many years in the navy you respect the weather. Your life may depend on it."

Katie waved good night. As she walked back to Lavender Cottage, she couldn't remember ever feeling so content. But having spent months on a roller coaster she wondered if she was experiencing the calm before the storm or was that behind her.

A tremendous thud woke Katie, she glanced at the clock 2 a.m. Buddy sat up and gave a woof. The wind howled around the cottage and rain hammered on the window. Bob was right. She peered out of the window but it was black. She followed Buddy downstairs to find the source of the thud. Lights shone through the lounge window; she saw Mary and Bob in the lane shinning flashlights on an oak tree sprawled across the road. Katie pulled on her wellington boots and raincoat. Buddy gave her an odd look. She laughed. "No Buddy, no walks in the middle of the night but something has happened at Mary and Bob's place. You stay like a good boy."

Katie braced herself against the wind. The tree had fallen across the road and a large branch had pierced Mary's front window. They were trying to move the tree to get the branch out of the window.

Katie yelled, "Can I help!"

"Gives us a hand with this." Bob pointed to the tree. The three heaved and the tree wouldn't budge. "We need more man power." He had no sooner said the words than several bright yellow raincoats appeared from the cottages at the top of Marina Lane. Henry arrived with a large chain saw.

"Bob, lets chop the branch off. We'll never move the whole tree."

"Okay, then I can pull the branch from the window."

Half an hour later the offending branch was pulled away from the window and a large tarp was fastened over the gapping hole to keep out the rain.

"Leave the rest until daylight." Bob shouted over the wind. "Thanks everyone!"

Astonished that everyone knew what to do, Katie watched as people just appeared when needed. She wondered if that would have happened on Autumn Road and sadly the answer was no, except for Phil, he always helped.

Lavender Cottage stood next to Marine Cottage, Mary and Bob's place, and Katie took a walk around the property to make sure nothing had fallen on her cottage. Had the tree fallen to the left it would have hit Katie's roof.

Chainsaws whined as Bob and Henry cut the massive tree in pieces. The rain had stopped, but the wind howled blowing into every nook and cranny of the old cottage. Katie shivered pulling a thick Arran knit sweater over her blouse.

"Come Buddy, lets see if we can help Mary." Walking towards Marine Cottage, Bob called, "She's at the café."

"Thanks!" Katie yelled over the wind and ran to the café, tying Bud to the porch railing for shelter. Buddy shivered. "Hey, none of that or I'll buy you one of those doggie coats." As if he knew what she was saying he sat down and lifted his chin in the air. Katie ruffled his head and entered the café.

"Take a seat. We're behind today." Mary called over her shoulder.

"I thought you'd be closed because of the damage to your cottage."

"No, I never close except for Christmas Day."

"I'm here to help, not eat," Katie replied.

"Thanks, I could do with some help. I've got a big order going out this morning and I am so behind. Are you any good at baking?"

"I love baking."

"Good. The batter is in the mixer and the oven will be hot by the time the timer goes off on the mixer. When it stops, fill the muffin tins, paper cups are on the shelf, tins underneath. I'll make coffee because these big espresso machines are temperamental if you don't know what you're doing."

Katie pulled off her sweater and tied an apron around her waist as she walked into the back room, "Oh my," she said under her breath. The mixer came up to her chest and the mixing bowl was bigger than a rain barrel. She watched the beige and orange batter whirl around, *Carrot muffins, I'd better get on and do this* she thought pulling the muffin tins from the shelf. The mixer beeped and stopped. She pushed and pulled but couldn't figure out how to lift the bowl out.

"Sorry to disturb you, Mary, but how do you get this bowl out?"

Mary flipped a knob on the side and the beaters lifted up, freeing the bowl for Mary to wheel it to the counter.

"Well, how neat is that?" Katie said.

"That bowl is too heavy to lift when its full so it sits on a cradle with wheels."

"There's a lot of batter here? Will you sell all these muffins in one day?"

"Cyril has an auction this morning up at the antique shop and I provide coffee and muffins mid-morning. He gets nasty if I'm late."

"I met him at the pub last night. He tried to sell me some paintings. He's a tad full of himself."

"That's Cyril! He fell on hard times early in life and has a chip as big as a log on his shoulder. He's a mystery. No one knows where he came from, except that he's not from around here. But he's a darn good auctioneer, and he knows his antiques. He moved here the same time we did. There," Mary said, filling the last muffin cup. "Open the oven doors and I'll put the trays in. Blueberry next, Cyril's favourite."

"What do you think of Maisie?" Mary asked as she emptied a bag of flour into the mixer and scooped raw eggs from a bucket. "Grab the sugar on the scale and pour it in here."

"Well, she's a character, but I liked her. At first I thought 'typical barmaid,' but she's more than that."

"You're a good judge of character. She's a business woman. Even when Bill was alive, she ran the show. Maisie helped us set up this business. Stevie, her son, is a great kid, but slow. He took it hard when his dad died. Bob has him over at the marina as often as Maisie allows." Mary giggled. "Maisie doesn't give him much time off."

Katie couldn't believe how many muffins they baked, scones they rolled, and sandwiches they cut in less than two hours. That included serving customers, although it was a slow morning due to the storm.

"It's time to go to Cyril's. Would you mind watching the shop while I deliver this?" Mary pointed to the van outside the back door, loaded with coffee and muffins. "Bob's the delivery man but he needs to get that tree off the road. They've cleared a narrow path so I can get the van through."

"Okay, I can do that."

Katie stood at the counter, grinning. She felt like a kid playing at shop. Several boaters came in for coffee, checking their boats after the storm. As the door opened a third time, she heard Buddy bark. "Oh dear. Buddy, I forgot all about you. Wait until Mary gets back."

"Do you talk to yourself often?"

She looked up from the coffee machine to see Piers standing at the counter. "No, well, sometimes. I came to give Mary a hand. A tree came down last night and broke Mary's living room window and I forgot all about Buddy."

"Buddy is fine. He was barking at Arthur." Piers gave her a tender reassuring smile. "It must have been a big storm to bring an oak down. I'll have a coffee and carrot muffin to go, please? It was bad in Nottingham too, lots of flooding from the rain."

Handing him a paper bag, she added, "I baked those this morning." Katie's cheeks reddened as she realized her pride in the muffins was childish. What was it about the man that made her spin? "You're not working today?"

"Later. I don't start until one so I came to check the boat."

"Bob checked everything last night. I was taking a walk before the storm started. Where do you…" she wanted to ask him where he worked but Bob walked in, asking for coffees for the men working on the tree.

"I'm taking Arthur for a walk. Can Buddy come?"

"Yes, thank you." She turned to Bob. "How many coffees?"

"Six please and give me a bag of muffins. It's hungry work."

Katie picked up a tray and placed the coffees with milk and sugar, and a bag of muffins on it. "You're a natural, Katie. Thanks for helping Mary. She hates to be late opening up but that storm really upset her." The back door slammed in the wind. "She's back. Everything okay, love?" Bob yelled.

"All good," Mary said, stepping behind the counter. "Cyril's got a big crowd. I thought the storm might put people off but he must have something special today. I see the tree has gone."

"We're finished. I just need to stack the wood. Katie, would you like some?"

"Please. I am enjoying the fireplace."

"I'll stack it between the cottages and you can help yourself. It's better to let the wood dry before burning it though." Bob leaned over the counter and gave Mary a peck on the cheek.

Katie ordered her favourite, the chicken special with salad. Hungry after a morning's work, she sat at a table and enjoyed lunch before going shopping. Too tired to go far, she decided to try the general store for a few essentials and to meet the Johnsons.

Eleven

Christmas is Coming!

A bowl of water and a large stone lay on the ground under the window of the General Store and Post Office. Katie tied Buddy's leash around the stone *I love that the village is dog friendly and it usually means people friendly too,* she thought, as Buddy lapped at the bowl of water. His walk with Piers and Arthur had made him thirsty.

The bell jangled as she opened the door but the shop appeared empty and quiet. The smell of not-so-fresh vegetables, ground coffee and cheese hit her nostrils. "Hello?" she called, her eyes scanning the shelves of Heinz baked beans, tinned peas, corned beef and spam. A large round of cheese sat on a wooden board with a wire and handle, something she hadn't seen since a child. Wilted lettuce, bruised tomatoes and half a cucumber lay on a vegetable stand with carrots, turnips and potatoes. Plastic wrapped slice bread, packaged cakes and crumpets lined the shelf below the canned goods.

"Hello," Katie called again, wishing she'd picked up bread from Mary's and not sure she wanted to buy anything in the store.

Gladys Johnson appeared from behind a curtained doorway and made a large puffing entrance, the emphasis on large. She clutched her chest to catch her breath. "Sorry love, hoo! I was upstairs." Her eyes rolled upwards, "We live in the flat above the shop and Dan's gone to the wholesaler." Gladys wafted her hands, the excess flesh below her upper arm wobbled like a turkey's gizzard as she coughed. "Give me a minute." She took an inhaler from under the counter and held her breath as the medication calmed her breathing.

Katie frowned. "Are you all right?"

Gladys took a slow breath. "Yes. I have asthma and if I rush it sets me off coughing. I'm okay now."

Katie stifled a grin at the word 'rush'. Gladys' entrance had been dramatic but not rushed.

"Katie Saunders. You bought Adam's place, right? What can I get you?"

"Word travels fast in a small village." Katie said "I'll take half a pound of that cheese, a loaf of bread and a package of crumpets." *Crumpets and tea by the fire this afternoon,* she mused. "A pint of milk and do you have yogurt?"

"In the cooler, love." Gladys cut a hunk of cheese while Katie inspected the cooler, picking up milk, yogurt and butter.

"And I'll take a pound of coffee. That'll do me for now."

Gladys ground the coffee in an old and noisy machine and packed the groceries in a plastic bag, suggesting Katie bring a shopping bag next time. *If there is a next time,* Katie thought. She wanted to support local business, but the food was not fresh and very expensive. The bell jangled as she said goodbye to Gladys.

Buddy was curled up in the sun, taking a nap and not anxious to leave his comfy spot. Picking up his leash, Katie glanced up Main Street and saw the sign for the antique store on the corner near the by-pass. On a whim, she decided to check out Springsville Antiques.

Cyril was standing outside the store, smoking a cigarette. "Ms. Saunders, did you come to view the paintings?"

"Paintings?"

"The ones I mentioned at the pub. Please tie your dog up over there. I don't want any leg-lifting on my store front or furnishings."

"No problem." *Not so dog friendly here,* she thought and added, "I'm looking for two chairs for my lounge to go with my couch. It's mushroom coloured so anything will go with it."

"*Beige,*" Cyril said with a sneer. "I don't carry *beige.* Follow me."

Cyril led the way through the store full of beautiful old wooden tables, dressers and dining chairs. He entered an even larger room of easy chairs and couches of all styles, shapes, colours and sizes. Katie loved old furniture and he had several exquisite pieces.

Two rich royal blue, well-stuffed easy chairs caught her eye. The overstuffed back and sides engulfed her as she sank into its warm coziness. She flipped off her shoes and curled her legs underneath her.

"I love the bright cheerful blue. I'll put yellow cushions on them. Perfect for the morning room and the others can go back to the lounge. How much?"

"£650 for the pair and £750 with the ottoman."

"Wow! This is an expensive village." She glanced at her

plastic bag of groceries.

"Did you shop at Gladys' place? How they stay in business, selling rotting vegetables, is a mystery. But the cheese is very good."

Ignoring his comment about Gladys' shop, she blurted out, "£400 with the ottoman."

"Please, Ms. Saunders don't insult me. These chairs may be used but they are in perfect condition and made by one of the best high quality manufactures. They will last forever. £650 and I'll throw in the ottoman for free."

Katie mused over the price. The chairs she liked, but she didn't need the ottoman. "£500 and no ottoman. I can buy new chairs in Nottingham for that price."

"Not the same quality." Cyril hesitated. "£550 with the ottoman. It's no good to me without the chairs."

Katie thought for a minute. Cyril was right. A bright blue ottoman would be difficult to sell without the chairs. "£525 for all three pieces and that is my final offer."

Cyril's mouth curled into a wry smile. "Okay, Ms. Saunders, you drive a hard bargain. I'm surprised I..."

"You assumed I'd be a push over. A few months ago, you would have been right."

"£525 it is, but only because you're new to the village and I like you." Cyril offered his hand and they shook to seal the deal. "If Stevie is free, I can deliver them this afternoon. Maisie's son is a strong lad and good with deliveries."

Katie bounced along Main Street, happy with her chairs and ottoman purchase. She took the shortcut through the village green and let Buddy have a run.

True to his word, Cyril arrived with Stevie and they moved the mushroom coloured chairs into the lounge. Katie saw Cyril give them a look of disdain. Stevie carried the new chairs with ease through the wide French doors and placed them each side of the fireplace with the ottoman in the centre. Katie gave Cyril a cheque and Stevie a £5 note as a tip. He smiled and made eye contact, with lovely, gentle blue eyes. "Thank you," Stevie said, his eyes returning to his feet.

Buddy curled up on his bed, exhausted from all the walks, while Katie lit a fire and made tea and toasted crumpets. She placed the tray on the ottoman and curled her legs underneath her on the new chair. Opening her book, she sipped tea and relished the warm buttery crumpets. "Does life get any better than this?"

Katie's book slipped to the floor and she woke with a start. A voice called, "Knock, knock. Anyone home?"

"Phil, how lovely to see you."

"The storm hit hard around here, I wanted to make sure you were okay and Melanie asked me to check on you."

"I'm fine." Katie gave him a puzzled look. "Melanie?"

"We kept in touch by email. She's concerned as she hasn't received an email from you since you moved."

"The internet is not set up."

"I can do that for you. I just need your username and password."

"Thank you! It's on that card by the laptop."

Phil opened her laptop and pressed a few keys. "All done. I had dinner with Anne and Dave last night. Dave talked of the scandal at Becket Marketing and I have news about Brianna."

"I don't care." Just the mention of her name had given Katie a jolt, intruding on her new-found happiness.

"You'll be interested in this. Becket fired her and, desperate for money, she sold her house. Lost a bundle for a quick sale and disappeared with no forwarding address."

"I still don't care."

Phil continued and Katie was getting annoyed. "The staff at Becket's is sorry for the way they treated you. They want to apologize. Sylvie Vickers is particularly sorry and wants you to consider coming back to work."

"That will never happen but I'm gratified that the truth is revealed. Sylvie never believed the rumours and I liked her. We could have been friends but I couldn't work near Graham again. Besides, I love it here. I even worked in the bakery this morning."

Phil stayed for most of the evening. They talked, drank wine and ate Gladys' cheese, which turned out to be excellent. Phil spoke about Melanie, making Katie wonder if a romance was brewing. But she dismissed the thought as long distance relationships don't generally work, so it was unlikely they would ever be more than friends with similar interests.

Adam came to visit twice a week and Katie began to notice how his trousers bunched up where he'd pulled his belt tight, his jacket hung off his shoulders and every time he came, his face was paler. It was the day before Christmas Eve and he was rocking away talking to Doris and crying. As soon as the back door opened, Buddy ran out and sat at Adam's feet. "Doris, I can't do it anymore. I want to be with you." His back shook with sobs.

Katie walked up to him and placed her hand on his shoulder. "Adam, what's wrong? What has upset you so?"

It wasn't Adam that spoke but Doris. *'Sonia is making Adam's life hell.'* Her voice quivered and Katie thought, if ghosts could cry Doris was crying.

"I'm sorry. I'll try to help him." Katie wasn't sure what she could do. But she could talk to Kevin when he came to pick him up? "Doris, it's cold out here. Adam's shivering and he needs to get warm."

Katie helped Adam inside and gave him a hug. "Adam, please tell me what's going on. I can help."

"I don't like to speak ill of family. I'm all right."

"No, you're not! Tell me what's going on."

"Kevin brings me tea and biscuits in the morning before he goes to work." He sniffed and wiped his nose. "Sonia won't allow me downstairs for breakfast or lunch while she's working in her office. If I venture downstairs, she punches me in the arm and screams at me to go to my room." He rolled his sleeve up to revealed big bruises on his arm. "That was because I was hungry and came to get a snack on Sunday. I assumed Kevin was home. I'm allowed to come downstairs if Kevin is home."

"Does Kevin know? Or is he part of it?"

"Oh, no!"

"You have to tell him."

"It will upset him. Sonia can do nothing wrong in Kevin's eyes. She was in a bad marriage before she met Kevin and he's very protective."

"Oh! Is Christina from her first marriage?"

"Yes and she's a spoiled brat. But if Kevin tries to discipline her, Sonia goes into a rage."

"Oh dear. It doesn't sound like a happy home."

"Doris and I felt sorry for her at first. She told us that her ex-husband abused her and the little girl. She's quite an actress. Kevin bought into it as well. Doris had doubts even before they married, but we didn't understand what she was like until

I lived there."

Adam felt better after talking to Katie and he settled by the fire, reading and snoozing while Katie baked shortbread, the last of the Christmas baking.

Katie and John had made a big thing of Christmas, not just for the kids, but for neighbours and friends but this year would be different. It would be the first Christmas without John and it occurred to her that Ben wouldn't be there either. She wasn't sure what to expect.

Melanie was due to arrive that night. Phil was picking her up from the airport and they were both staying over the holiday. Life had changed. It was even true for Judy. Ever since her divorce, she and her sons had spent Christmas with Katie and John. But this year Judy would be coming alone as the boys had other plans. Judy had brushed it off but she couldn't hide her sadness from her best friend. Mary and Bob were invited to join them for Christmas dinner and anyone else who might be alone but most village folks, except the Binghams, had an extended family. *No wonder I feel apprehensive about Christmas. But, whatever happens I will enjoy this.* Adam's voice shook her from her thoughts.

"Kevin's here." Adam called, gathering his things.

"Hello Kevin, your dad is all ready. Are you prepared for Christmas?"

"I'm a last-minute guy. I'm taking Dad shopping on our way home. You look pale, Dad? Are you unwell?" Kevin patted his arm and Katie saw a controlled wince.

Adam gave Katie a quick glance. "I'm fine. Let's get going. I have serious shopping to do."

"Kevin, take care of your father and spend time with him. He misses your mum." As much as Katie worried, she didn't have time to deal with the problem right now. She had considered inviting Adam's family, but the thought of entertaining Sonia put her off.

Kevin gave her a quizzical glance that told her he'd sensed there was more meaning to her comment. He hesitated but like everyone else the day before Christmas Eve, he had things to do and led Adam to the car. She'd talk to Kevin after the holidays.

The car pulled up to the curb and Katie watched as her daughter climbed out and Phil opened the trunk to get the luggage. Her heart leaped out of her chest as she recognized the tall young man unfolding from the back seat. Ben was home. She ran along the path, tears streaming. "Ben, oh Ben! What a wonderful surprise!" She looked at Melanie. "You kept this a secret?"

"Ben emailed, two days ago, to ask what time I was arriving. It turned out his plane arrived one hour before mine. Here we are."

Katie was on tiptoes hugging Ben and released him to hug Melanie. Ben picked up his guitar and a backpack. "It's good to home. I like the look of your new digs."

Another car parked behind Phil as Judy and two retrievers arrived. The group huddled, greeted, hugged and everyone talked at once as they moved towards the cottage.

Katie settled everyone in a room and made dinner. Unable to hide her joy she said, "This will be a good Christmas." Lavender Cottage rang out with abundant Christmas cheer.

On Christmas Day, Katie needed a break and took Buddy for a walk along the towpath while Judy took Lily and Sam into the field. Holding her hand out to catch feathery snowflakes, she called to Judy, "Snow on Christmas Day is perfect. See you back at the cottage."

On the way back, she saw a light on at *Tranquil Days*. Afraid someone had broken in, she peered through the window and came face to face with Piers. Embarrassed, she jumped back as he appeared through the hatch.

"Piers, I am so sorry. I saw the light and was afraid someone might have broken in." Buddy jumped on the boat to greet Arthur and Katie shouted at him to return.

"I came to check on things," Piers said, his voice flat. He appeared lost and his usual confidence had disappeared.

"Happy Christ… mas," Katie said with hesitation, realizing he was alone. "Are you by yourself?"

"Just me and Arthur." He cleared his throat and stared at the water. "We're heading back to town. I don't celebrate Christmas."

"If you have time, why don't you come and have a drink or join us for dinner? Mary and Bob are coming. Both my children came home for Christmas. Melanie met Ben at the airport. What a wonderful…" Katie stopped as Piers eyes were glassy and wet and the colour had drained from his face.

"Thank you but I'm meeting friends in Nottingham. In fact, I need to lock up and leave." Piers bent down and returned to the cabin, leaving Katie staring at an empty space and Arthur whining at the closed hatch. She shuddered. Something was wrong. Or was she sticking her nose where it didn't belong? The hatch opened and closed as Arthur disappeared into the cabin.

"Come, Buddy. We have a turkey to carve."

One day merged into the next over the holiday. Mary and Bob pretty much adopted Melanie and Ben as part of their family. Melanie and Phil's friendship seemed to be natural as though they belonged together. Katie sensed something more than friendship was developing but she couldn't be sure. They drank wine and ate copious amounts of turkey, Christmas pudding and shortbread. Ben played his guitar as they sang carols. Katie felt tears of joy with her home full of love and laughter once again. John never entered her mind but Piers did. His behaviour troubled her, especially since he didn't return to town. His car never moved from the parking lot. Whatever was wrong, he was keeping it to himself.

Twelve

The Worst Winter Storm

The drive to the airport was sombre as Katie struggled to hold back tears in the back seat. *Why do my children have to be globetrotters? Ben will disappear into the United States to play music and Melanie into the forests of Peru.* She brushed her cheeks and stared at the road ahead. Phil glanced at Melanie in the front seat and stretched his arm across to hold her hand. Melanie gave him a gentle, loving smile. *Ah, so romance is in the air! If I'm right, Melanie might come home.*

Ben touched her arm. "Mum, don't be sad. We've had a wonderful Christmas." He sat forward in the seat and turned to face Katie. "I need to tell you something."

Katie held her breath. "Are you in trouble?"

"No, the opposite. I'm serious about music. While touring around America, I met up with a bunch of talented jazz musicians and helped them organize a successful tour. We met one of your favourite singers, Diana Krall, a famous Canadian jazz singer. She was impressed by the band and introduced us to a recording studio in New York who offered the band a record label. The band asked me to be their manager. I just applied for my Green Card so I can stay in America."

"This is good news."

"I'll still come home for visits. It'll be even easier when we tour Europe. And as soon as I find an apartment, you can come and visit me in New York."

Katie wanted to ask a million questions, but knowing Ben that was all the information he'd share. She kissed his cheek. "I'm proud of you, son. I've always wanted to visit New York. Have you told your father?"

"No. I don't need his lectures. I want nothing to do with him." Ben stared out of the side window.

The car slowed as they entered the departure section of East Midlands Airport. It wasn't a metropolis, but a convenient way of getting to London Heathrow.

Melanie and Ben waved goodbye as they wheeled their luggage into the terminal. After they disappeared, Katie slipped into the front seat and Phil pulled the car onto the main road, heading back to Springsville.

"You have a wonderful family. Ben is quite a character. I admire his free spirit but I'm not sure I could live with such uncertainty."

"Ben has always been different but he's found his calling at last. He's going to manage a jazz band in New York. Things will work out this time. I just wish it wasn't the other side of the Atlantic."

"Melanie has spirit too, in a scientific way. It takes courage to take your science to a foreign country. I am fascinated by the project and find my teachings on environment at the college somewhat boring in comparison. She's is a wonderful person. I'm fond of her...in a friendly way." His cheeks glowed very slightly.

As they turned into Marina Lane, he spoke again. "Here we are. I'll drop you off and be on my way. Thank you for including me in your family Christmas. I had a wonderful time."

"I enjoyed having you. You have no family?"

"None to speak of." He paused. "It's a long story for another time." He gave her an affectionate smile that didn't quite meet his eyes.

"Well, thanks for driving me home. Pop by anytime."

Little Christmas, January 5th, was the day tradition dictated Christmas decorations be removed. Someone, somewhere, said that leaving them past this date was bad luck. Katie smiled, not sure she believed in such sayings. But it was a convenient date to put everything away. She unhooked the baubles from the tree and packed them away with memories of a wonderful Christmas; different memories but loving ones that lingered on. Her home had once again been full of love and laughter. She liked having the company. The quiet was lonely and maybe she needed more to fill her days.

Buddy woofed at the front door and Katie opened it but there was no one there. She stepped outside to see Judy's SUV turn the corner on to Marina Lane. "How do you do that? Anticipate Judy's arrival before we can see her," she said, patting his head. He wagged his curly tail, sat on his haunches and waited for the car to pull up. Lily and Sam jumped out of the car and the three had a great reunion. Judy and Katie laughed at the antics. Buddy loved to run underneath the retrievers' bellies and it drove Lily crazy trying to find him. Sam usually ignored him.

Judy pulled the ladder down from the attic and climbed to the top, surprised to find a whole expanse of storage space. She stacked the boxes and pulled herself into the attic as Katie put her head through the opening.

"Wow! I could use the space for extra storage. It looks as though Adam left things behind, though." She bent down under the eaves and brushed dust off an old trunk and several boxes stacked next to it. "He must have forgotten he had stuff in here."

"It's cold up here." Judy shivered as she climbed onto the attic ladder. "Time for a glass of wine. I brought your favourite Merlot." Katie followed, folding the ladder up into the attic trap door.

Judy poured the wine and Katie climbed over Lily and Sam, sprawled out by the hearth to poke the fire. After puffing up the yellow cushions, Katie tucked her legs on the seat and Judy stretched hers on the ottoman as they both relaxed in the comfy blue chairs.

Judy twisted her fingers around the stem of the wine glass. "I had a lovely Christmas, Katie. Thank you. I missed the boys but not as much as if I'd been alone."

"Lavender Cottage lends itself well to a big family gathering. I'm glad you were here. I'm not sure what I'll do with myself now. Ben won't be home for a long time. Melanie, I'm not sure. She and Phil are close. Do you think there's a budding romance?"

"Isn't it obvious?" Judy rolled her eyes. "Phil and Melanie make a great couple. Sometimes I wonder about you, my friend," Judy squeezed Katie's hand. "So what will you do with yourself? There aren't many jobs around here."

Katie nodded and sighed. "I wondered if Mary needed help in the bakery but probably not in the winter."

Judy cleared her throat and took a breath before speaking. "The cottage is ideal for a bed-and-breakfast, especially in the summer."

"Invite strangers in my house? No. I'd be uncomfortable, wondering if I was harbouring rapists or murderers."

"Really!" Judy laughed. "That's highly unlikely. What about renting out the suite?"

"That crossed my mind when I bought the place. A tenant with good references maybe? That, I would consider."

Judy stood up and picked up her handbag. "Time to go. I'm off to Manchester tomorrow for a week, working on a new bank building. Dad will take Lily and Sam again. I've been out of town so much in the last six months I feel guilty leaving them, but Dad says he likes the company."

"If ever you're stuck, I can take care of the dogs. Hey, you could sell your house, rent the suite and never worry about the dogs again."

"Sorry, I like my big house. But I might take you up on the dog sitting offer if Dad can't do it sometime. Thanks for everything. I'm off!"

The bedroom was dark when she woke, the clock reading 9 a.m. She flipped on the light and looked again. 9:01 She'd overslept. Katie stretched and glanced at the window, seeing a dark slate grey sky, heavy with snow. The howling wind rattling the windows had woken her. She dressed in the warmest cloths she could find, just as the doorbell rang. Adam walked in and Kevin shouted from the car window. "I'm running late! We slept in. I'll see you tonight."

"It's so dark," Katie said as she waved back.

Adam started the fire while she made coffee and breakfast. They ate and watched the snow fall. Within minutes, the wind blew the snow into ripples and small drifts. Buddy ran off into the garden and rolled around in the fresh snow.

It continued into the early afternoon. "I'm going to the marina. I doubt Mary opened the café today. Adam, will you stay by the fire? I won't be gone long."

The snow must have been six inches deep and more where the wind blew it into drifts. Buddy jumped, rather than walked, as his little legs sank into the snow past his belly. It had settled on low bushes and with no footprints or car tracks, it looked beautiful. When she reached the canal basin, it was an amazing site. The white snow against the coloured narrowboats and the water shimmering with a layer of ice made a beautiful contrast. It was quiet and still and she held her breath, afraid to disturb the silence.

A light shone from the café window and the bell jingled as Katie popped her head around the door. "Just making sure you're okay."

"Hello, Katie. Yes we're fine. No customers today. I got caught up and Bob's checking the boats. He's inspecting the ice. If it gets too thick, he has to break it or it will cause damage. Piers from *Tranquil Days* is helping him."

"He's a strange one. I invited him to join us Christmas Day. He said he had plans, but he stayed on the boat all week."

"He bought the boat about three years ago. At first, he kept to himself, one of those recluse types. It was just him and his dog, Arthur. He always looked sad but this last year he's come into the café a few times and talks to the other boaters. He seems like a nice guy but I still know nothing about him or even where he's from."

"He's from Nottingham but that's all I know. Can I help with anything?"

"No, I'm about to pack up. Here, take this apple pie and these scones. They'll be no good tomorrow."

"Thank you. Adam is visiting and he'll enjoy the pie."

Mary locked up and they walked to the moorings where Bob was bashing the thick layer of ice with a long pole. Buddy shivered and lifted his paws because of the ice on them. Katie picked him up, balancing the pie with one hand, as Buddy sniffed at the box. "Bye!" Katie shouted. "If you need any help, give me a shout."

Buddy jumped down in the doorway. "Mary sent an apple pie and I'll make tea." Katie frowned. "Adam! Where are you?"

Katie put the pie in the kitchen and saw the backdoor open a jar. *He's talking to Doris,* she thought. "Adam, it's cold out..." Adam was not on the porch but Katie saw Doris' chair rocking.

"Doris, where did he go?"

'Just wondered off.'

"What happened?"

'He's unhappy and wants to join me but it's not his time yet. He wasn't himself today.' Katie listened to Doris sob.

"I'll look for him. He can't have gone far."

111

Thirteen

Adam Wanders Off

C losing the back door, Katie followed the footsteps in the snow but by the time she got to the road, the wind had whipped the snow into more drifts. There were no footprints, not even hers from ten minutes ago. She felt panic, not knowing in which direction to start. Adam didn't have his coat on and she had seen his shoes at the front door, which meant he was wearing slippers. She ran to the marina.

"Bob, Piers, I need help. Adam has disappeared."

"Disappeared! What do you mean?" Piers said.

"When I returned, the back door was ajar and footsteps led off the porch and then disappeared. I've no idea where he can be."

"Let's split up. Piers, you go down to Church Lane. I'll check on the docks and around the café. Katie, you take the towpath. It's sheltered so you might find footprints." Bob took a phone from his pocket and called Mary, asking her to go along Marina

Lane to Main Street. "Meet back here and if there's no sign of him, we'll call the police."

Katie's cheeks were stinging from the wind and she was grateful for the shelter of the hedge along the towpath but there were no footprints. She walked a few more yards but Adam had not been down there so she headed back to Marina Lane. *The village green*, she thought. *That's where he is. He walked off the porch and through the back gate. How stupid not to think of that first.* Katie ran as fast as the snow would allow, scanning the village green and the gardens that backed on to it. She gave a big sigh of disappointment. Adam was not there.

She met Mary, returning from Main Street, and they walked to the boats. Piers and Bob had had no luck either. Bob had already dialed 999 and a rescue team was on its way but it would take them half an hour to arrive. Bob went up to the cottages and rallied more residents to help, asking everyone to check their gardens and sheds.

Katie stood still. She heard water. Not a big splash but water on the side of a boat. "I hear something in the water," she yelled and waved towards the last boat in the basin. "Over here!" Bob arrived first and dropped to his knees with Piers as they tried to pull something from the water.

"I need blankets. Lots of them! Do you have a defibrillator?" Piers had rolled Adam on his side.

"Yes, I'll get it," Bob yelled. "And, Mary, get blankets."

Piers looked at Katie, "Can you go to my boat? In the cabin, there is a black bag in the cupboard, just inside the door."

As Katie returned, Adam let out a cough and water poured from his mouth. His body went limp and Piers pulled a stethoscope from the bag to listen. "He's not breathing." Piers attached the defibrillator to his chest and Adam's back arched.

His throat gurgled and he shivered violently as Mary covered him with blankets.

Piers looked worried. "Where's the ambulance? If it doesn't get here soon, we'll need to move him somewhere warm." He'd no sooner finished speaking than the wail of sirens drowned his words. The ambulance doors opened and a paramedic grabbed a bag. Seeing Piers, he said, "Dr. Bannister, what do we have here?" Piers related the happenings as a gurney appeared and Adam was lifted on to it. He followed the paramedics and climbed into the ambulance.

Katie phoned Kevin, who was leaving work, and told him there'd been an accident and Adam was on the way to the Derby Infirmary. She'd meet him there.

Her car skidded on the ice and snow and it was a blessing that few vehicles were on the road. Her heart pounded as she gripped the steering wheel, her fingernails digging into her palms. She was perched on the edge of the seat, leaning forward and trying to keep the wheels straight but the car started to slide, slowly at first. She remembered to turn into the skid but nothing happened. She could only watch the hedge get closer before there was a slight bump as the car mounted the grass verge and stopped. Katie leaned her forehead on the steering wheel and took several deep breaths.

The front wheels were on the snow-covered grass verge and she decided that if she reversed slowly, she would have enough traction to get back on the road. It worked and she straightened the car, thankful to see the main street ahead. Once she got to the main road into Derby, the roads were wet and slushy but drivable.

Kevin, pale and worried, was sitting next to Piers when Katie arrived. He jumped up. "They won't tell me much. Piers said, he's suffering from hypothermia. The cold stopped his heart and we'll have to wait. Katie, what happened?"

"I left him sitting by the fire, reading, while I went to see Mary and when I got back, he was gone. I followed his footsteps through the garden but the wind covered them with snow. I found Bob and Piers at the dock and we began to search for him."

"Why did he leave the house?" Kevin asked.

Katie thought for a minute. Was this a god time tell him about Doris, that his dad was unhappy. She noted that she still hadn't told Kevin about the bruises on his arms.

"Is there something you're not telling me?" Kevin frowned, his head to one side.

"Your dad said odd things today. He said he was unhappy and that he wanted to join Doris."

"He won't talk to me, but his behaviour has been odd. He stays in his room all the time. He never goes out to play darts anymore and he seems nervous. He doesn't even eat much. He never used to be like that."

"I had intended to speak with you after the holiday. I'm not sure how to tell you this, but your dad is afraid of Sonia."

Kevin scoffed. "Don't be ridiculous!"

"Mr. Cummings!" A white-coated doctor approached Kevin. "Your father will be okay. The shock of the cold water stopped his heart, but thanks to Dr. Bannister's quick action, there's no damage. We still have tests to run. Other than that, and the hypothermia, he is strong for a seventy-five-year-old."

"That is good news. Can I see him?"

"I have a few questions first. Can you tell me what happened?"

"No, he was visiting Katie." Kevin led the doctor to Katie and repeated the doctor's request.

"He was reading by the fire. I went to check on a neighbour and when I got back, he'd gone."

The doctor glanced from Kevin to Katie. "Has he wondered off before or does he seem confused?" They both shook their heads. "He has nasty bruises on his arms. Some are new, from the fall, but others are yellow, which means they are old. Is he falling a lot?"

Katie said nothing and Kevin looked surprised. "I didn't know about the bruising."

"We'll know more in a few days. You can see him now, but don't stay too long. He needs rest."

Adam lay on his back with blankets on top of him and wires running to beeping machines. His face had the look of opaque glass. At first, Katie thought he was dead as he didn't move, or even blink.

"Hey Dad," Kevin whispered. "How are you feeling?"

Adam moved his eyes and the corners of his mouth twitched. "Son, I'm so cold. I wanted to go to your mother. I'm sorry." He moved his head towards Katie. "I'm sorry I scared you, Katie, but I told Doris I was coming."

Katie went to his bedside and held his hand. "I bet Doris told you not to." He gave her a weak smile. "She wants you to get better and enjoy a few more years." She bent down and kissed his forehead.

"I'm tired and cold. My eyes won't stay open."

"I'll wait outside." Katie left the room and to her surprise, Kevin followed her after a minute.

"He's asleep. Is he going crazy? Does he have... dementia? What's all this talk about my mum?"

"He likes to talk to your mum on the porch. He misses her

116

but he's not crazy, just sad and lonely. Kevin, he stays in his room because Sonia won't let him come downstairs when you're not there. He's losing weight since he isn't allowed lunch or even breakfast after you've gone to work. As for the bruises the doctor mentioned, Sonia punches him if he tries to go into the kitchen. I am sorry, but you need to talk to your wife."

"There has to be a misunderstanding. I know Sonia isn't too keen on having Dad but I find it hard to believe she would hurt him."

"Something has to be done, Kevin."

"I'll talk to Sonia and get her side of the story. I need to get home now. Thanks for your help."

Katie walked to Piers. "You're still here?"

"I was hoping you would offer me a lift to Springsville."

"Oh dear, sorry, I forgot you came in the ambulance. Here," Katie handed him the keys, "I hate driving in bad weather. Will you drive?"

The roads had had been cleared of snow on the way home and Katie sat back, tired after the drama but pleased that she had told Kevin about Sonia. She hoped he would do something and Adam would be okay.

"What was the doctor talking about? Bruising on Adam's arm?"

"Kevin's wife doesn't like him and she hits him. I knew about it before Christmas. I told Kevin tonight but I'm not sure he'll do anything."

"Well, if the authorities get involved, they could be in trouble."

"Perhaps they need to get involved. Then she would have to stop abusing Adam. I didn't realize that you are a doctor. Do

117

you work at the hospital in Nottingham?"

"When I come down to the boat, I leave my medicine behind." Piers hesitated. "I'm a GP in Nottingham. I used to work in emergency in both Derby and Nottingham but I gave that up three years ago. That's how Tim, the paramedic, knew me. I…" He hesitated and Katie gave an involuntary shudder, sensing something intense. "I needed to cut my workload down. I couldn't work for a while and I took on a partner, a younger man. He held the fort for me and when I came back to work part-time, he stayed on."

"That explains why I see you on your boat during weekdays. Are you better now? Was it a serious illness?"

"What? No, I'm not ill. Life sometimes throws you difficult curves. What about you? Tell me how you came to Springsville."

Katie prattled on about John and the kids, divorce and suburbia until they arrived at Marina Lane. She had done all the talking and other than discovering he was a doctor, Piers remained a mystery.

Buddy welcomed Katie with a rapid tail wag but he seemed agitated. She picked him up and frowned. "What's up, Bud?" Then she heard it, rhythmical banging getting louder. She froze and was about to run after Piers, thinking there was an intruder in the cottage. Before she could, Buddy wiggled out of her arms and ran to the back door. As soon as she stepped into the kitchen, she knew what the sound was. Doris in the rocking chair was frantic to know where and if they'd found Adam.

"Doris, you're making a lot of noise. Adam is fine. He fell into the narrowboat basin and has hypothermia. He is in hospital and doing okay."

Doris's voice quivered more than usual, *I had a glimpse of him. His arms were reaching for me, which meant he had died but then he disappeared. It's not his time yet.'*

"The shock of the cold water stopped his heart for a few minutes so maybe that's when you saw him. Dr. Bannister got it going again. Adam will be in hospital a few days. I talked to Kevin too, and told him how Sonia was treating him. He said he'd to talk to her. "

'Ask him to come and stay with you when he gets out of hospital. He'll need looking after and I don't trust Sonia.'

"If Kevin is okay with it, he can come here and stay in the suite upstairs. I'd like the company." Doris's chair slowed down and then stopped. "Bye," Katie whispered.

The next morning the temperature rose above freezing but it rained. Despite the new boiler, Katie found it cold and damp during the day. She lit both fires before Kevin arrived, bearing good news about Adam.

"How's he doing?"

"Very well. I spent most of the day at the hospital with him. He was chatting and joking, just like he used to do. The tests results are good and he'll be home in a day or two."

"That is excellent news."

Kevin cleared his throat. "Katie, I talked to Sonia about Dad and she admitted, not to hitting him, but in her words, tapping his arm to get his attention. She said he was difficult and interrupted her work. She's a business consultant and works from home."

Katie realized he was making excuses for Sonia's behaviour and yet, he loved his father and had seen the change in him. She had to ask. "What are you going to do? Your dad will need care when he comes home. It's important that he avoids stress, eats well and gets proper rest and exercise. Do you think Sonia can do that?"

"No. I will take time off work but I can't do that for another week."

"Kevin, he will need extra care when he first comes home." Katie hesitated and remembered her promise to Doris. "How do you feel about him coming here?"

"He'd love that and it would solve a lot of problems."

"That's settled then. Can you pack him some clothes and personal things?"

"I'll bring them by tomorrow after I've visited Dad. Thank you, you are a life saver. It will give me a chance to sort out Sonia." He paused. "Things aren't good between us. There are times I think Mum was right." His voice dropped almost to a whisper, as if he realized some truths.

The next afternoon, much to Katie's surprise, Kevin not only dropped off Adam's things but Adam himself.

"I hope you don't mind that we're early. Dad wanted to come home," Kevin announced. "The doc said as long as he took it easy, there was no reason to keep him in hospital."

"Not at all. His room is ready and I'm making soup for dinner. Would you like to stay?"

"Thanks. It smells wonderful but I have to rush home. Bye Dad, I'll pop by after work in a few days."

As Kevin left, Bob called from the open front door. "Can I come in? I wondered how Adam was doing?"

"Me too." Piers' voice came behind Bob's.

"Goodness, this is Grand Union station today. Come in. Adam is in the morning room. I was just about to serve soup.

Would you like some?"

"Thanks, but no thanks. Mary's got a stew on today."

"Smells good," Piers said. "I'll take you up on the offer. The surgery was busy today, and I didn't get a chance to eat. I'll be back after I get Arthur from the car."

Buddy and Arthur chased around the garden and ate each other's food before curling up on Buddy's bed by the fire. Adam, Piers and Katie relished the homemade soup with some of Mary's crusty bread, perfect for a cold night.

Fourteen

The Promise of Snowdrops

꧁꧂

The January snow, more than the usual sprinkling, lingered all month with bitter cold winds but February brought warmer weather that melted the snow and ice. Adam, fully recovered from his ordeal, was showing no signs of returning to Kevin's house and Katie wasn't rushing him out the door. In fact, she enjoyed his company. Springsville was quiet in the winter and even Mary and Bob kept to themselves, mostly busy getting ready for the season. Judy and the retrievers came for their Saturday walks when she was working in town and their girlfriend chats kept Katie from complete boredom. Piers had been a regular visitor during Adam's recovery, but recently she had only seen him from a distance and she missed his company. They had talked about his work as a doctor; the importance of his patients and how he cared for them all like his own relations. Piers never spoke of family or his personal life. A few times, Katie sensed she was close, but he clamped up or changed the subject.

The warm sun hit her face as she opened the French doors to the rose garden and walked along the path. She was delighted to see a clump of snowdrops, their delicate white flowers bent towards the earth, encouraging its blossom into spring.

Adam followed, inspecting the roses. "The roses have wintered well but it's early days yet. There's still a potential for frost." He pointed to the garden beyond the lawn. "In a couple of weeks, that will be full of daffodils, tulips and hyacinths and as the scent of hyacinth fades, the lilacs will take their place."

"I love spring. It should be mandatory to celebrate it." Katie laughed. "Mary was telling me the village celebrates in August with the Rose Fete and I noticed everyone has roses in their garden."

"The Rose Fete is hundreds of years old. The soil here is perfect for them. I always entered the best bloom contest and I shall miss it this year."

Katie looked puzzled. "Don't you want to enter this year?"

"Yes, but they aren't my roses anymore."

"Would you enter my roses? If you nurture them for the contest, they would be your roses. My thumbs don't have even a hint of green."

Adam beamed. "I was hoping you would say that." Clearing his throat, he added, "there is something I wanted to ask you."

"Adam, what is it?" Concern filled Katie's voice.

"Lavender Cottage is still home and I want to stay here. I can pay rent."

"Adam, I love having you here and you are welcome to stay. What about Kevin, though? Is he okay with you living here?"

"I haven't mentioned it. They are talking about building a separate office for Sonia with a private entrance. Kevin wants me to be comfortable in the house but it wouldn't work because I'll never be comfortable with Sonia. I don't want him to go to the expense of building an addition."

"You are welcome to stay here. Why don't you invite Kevin to come for a beer at the Boater's Inn and discuss it over a game of darts?"

"Thank you. I'll do that today. He's coming by after work."

That night, Kevin agreed that Adam should take up permanent residence at Lavender Cottage. He loved his father and the hurt showed in his face but Katie also sensed the relief, knowing his wife would be happy with the arrangements. She refused any money but put Adam in charge of the garden in lieu of rent.

The marina came to life in March as Bob and Mary prepared for the spring. It never closed, but Easter marked the beginning of the boating season and March brought the spring garden to life. Katie wanted to pinch herself, brimming with happiness.

Adam was a perfect tenant. She loved having someone to nurture; something that had been missing from her life. She helped Mary at the bakery a couple of afternoons a week and Buddy enjoyed his daily walks along the towpath. She even learned to play darts and went to the pub with Adam on occasions. Adam had joined the darts league and played well. He even went on a tournament with the guys. Doris said he hadn't been that happy since before she fell ill and Katie had noticed he no longer used a walking stick and she reckoned he seemed ten years younger since he'd been living at Lavender Cottage.

Katie gave a shiver. A noise, a car or something, had woken her. She could hear the howling wind and rubbish blowing around. *March winds blow,* she thought and hoped it would ease up before Melanie's plane landed. Melanie's project in Peru was on hold because the university had run out of funds. The temporary professor had given notice and the dean had requested that Melanie return early to resume teaching. Disappointed, but grateful for what they had achieved in Peru, Melanie took the recall in her stride. Katie was over the moon to have her daughter home again; although home was in Nottingham, it was closer than Peru.

Eager to see her daughter, Katie had offered to pick her up at East Midlands but she had a ride and needed to attend a meeting at the university that evening. Katie suspected Phil was picking her up. She would have to be patient and wait until Melanie visited on Saturday.

Buddy trotted downstairs and Katie let him into the garden where the wind almost blew him over. She made coffee and lit a fire. Perhaps it would compensate for the howling outside.

Adam came downstairs, picked up his morning newspaper and a letter from the letter box. The wind had woken him early too.

"This is for you," he said handing her the white envelope with an ornate logo by the return address. "No stamp. Hand delivered. I didn't see it last night when I locked up."

The morning coziness changed. She didn't need to open the letter since the logo told her it was from John. It was probably John's car that had woken her. News from him was never good. *What now? Why can't you leave me alone? Am I being unfair?* He'd been cordial the last couple of times they had spoken even as he whined about paying the alimony he had no choice about.

"Unless you have x-ray eyes, you can't read through the envelope," Adam said, with a grin. When he saw Katie's pale face he added, "I'm sorry. Is this bad news?"

"It's from John, and I suspect it is." She gave an unhappy grin as she ripped the envelope.

Dear Katie,

I hope this letter finds you well and the kids are okay. I never hear from them. Perhaps you could remind them they have a father?

My life is not going too well. Crystal left me after maxing out my credit cards and I had to sell the loft, at a loss. I'm staying at a friend's until I can find a place to live. The partners ganged up on me, saying I wasn't pulling my weight and my client base has shrunk, reducing my income to a pittance.

Katie stopped reading. "It's always about him. No wonder the kids don't keep in touch," she whispered.

I can't pay any more alimony. This will be the last month. The solicitor has applied to the courts under the prevision of a change of circumstances. Your solicitor will be in touch. There is no point in fighting this as I'm broke and even the courts can't get blood out of stone. I suggest you save your money for living expenses instead of on expensive lawsuits. I understand you are working part-time now so your situation has changed too.

Anger bubbled to the surface; she wanted to punch him. John

had spent all of *their* money and most of it *she* had saved to invest for their retirement. In less than a year, he had spent it on a fancy loft, a sports car, expensive women and Caribbean holidays with nothing left to meet his obligations. Part of her wanted to say 'serves you right' but she well knew how he would suffer with embarrassment. Appearances were important to John—she had a twinge of pity for him—then realized the impact on her income. Two afternoons a week on minimum wage would not pay the bills. How did he even find out she was working?

Katie was the money manager in the marriage and she had been careful after the divorce. John had not. She had money put aside but it wouldn't last long.

Adam's voice intruded on her thoughts. "Is it bad?"

"Yes, it is. John will stop paying alimony. It's not unexpected, but sooner than I hoped. When I bought this place, it seemed like the right thing to do. I was aware that a commute to work would be an issue but I didn't want to work, so I ignored it."

"Things will work out. First, I insist on paying rent at market value. No arguments!" Adam raised his voice and gave her a stern stare. Katie didn't dare disagree.

"You do so much for me. I'm uncomfortable charging rent but it would help. If Mary can add a few more hours at the bakery, I can scrape by." Katie paused. "Sylvie Vickers offered me my old job back. That paid well. It would mean driving to Milton every day but it's not as bad as Derby or Nottingham." Even saying the words made her uncomfortable. She did not want to work for Beckets again.

A wave of injustice swept over her and she wanted to weep. An hour ago, her life was happy and John had ruined it again. She heard a voice inside her giving her good advice. *Stop whining Katie, and stop blaming John for everything. Take charge of your life and that means supporting yourself. On the bright side, supporting yourself would forever break the ties from John.*

As expected, the solicitor called that morning and arranged an appointment for that same afternoon as there was some urgency.

Katie sat in the plush mahogany office as pound signs chinked in her head. Perhaps she needed to find a less fancy solicitor. So far, John had paid the fees, but she was on her own now. Mr. Clark was a kind man but his hourly rate was more than she earned in a month.

"Ms. Saunders, Mr. Saunders is asking for you to consider reconciliation."

Katie stared at him, her eyes almost popped out of her head. "I beg your pardon?"

Mr. Clark smiled. Katie wondered why a solicitor's smile was conciliatory and never reached their eyes. "That's what his solicitor is saying. I'm obliged to ask you if you want reconciliation."

"That's ridiculous! I moved on and built a new life for myself. My answer for the record is *no*. I am not interested in reconciliation."

"The law requires that I ask you if reconciliation is a possibility so I can record your answer."

"I had a letter from John this morning," Katie said. "He didn't mention reconciliation. He wants to stop paying alimony." Katie handed over the letter and watched him read it. His lips curled into a grin and this time the amusement spread through his face and into his eyes. Lovely deep blue eyes, she thought.

"My interpretation of the letter, combined with his request, is that he has nowhere to live and no money. He is trying to bully you into challenging him in court."

"I can't afford to challenge him. I will have to support myself but this was rather short notice."

"Mr. Saunders can't just stop paying. Either you come to a mutual agreement or the court decides whether a change is appropriate. Our reply will indicate that any change of circumstances must go through the proper channels." Mr. Clark glanced at Katie. "Ms. Saunders, he's playing games and looking for loopholes. Most ex-husbands resent paying alimony. It's a quick fix in early negotiations. Now, he's having serious regrets."

"Perhaps. But I've changed and moved on."

Mr. Clark moved to the door. "Leave it with me, Ms. Saunders. There's nothing to worry about."

Katie left the office in Milton and walked towards Becket Marketing. She hovered by the entrance, reluctant to even step inside. The door swung open while she waited, almost knocking her over.

"Katie, how lovely to see you," Sylvie said. "I was just going for coffee. Please join me?"

"Thank you," Katie said, wondering how she would explain hovering by the door.

The conversation over coffee was mostly about the scandal surrounding Brianna, Graham and his wife. Most of it she already knew and the rest was of no interest but it served to convince Katie that she did not want to work for Becket Marketing. When Sylvie asked, she had no trouble saying an emphatic *no*, and explained that she had a paying tenant and a part-time job at the bakery. She expected Sylvie to belittle her occupation but she didn't. Instead, she asked if she could come and visit. They parted friends and Katie invited her to pop by anytime.

She drove back to Springsville with a sense of pride. Without agonizing over the decision, she had calmly said no to Sylvie. Assessing her financial situation on the way home, she wondered if she'd been hasty. "No, this is a good decision. I can use my saving, if necessary," she said aloud, turning on to Marina Lane. Judy's car was in her driveway and two golden retrievers bounded out as Katie pulled in beside her friend.

"How lovely to see you! Are you staying for the weekend?"

"Is that okay? It's been a busy week I need some R-and-R. Where've you been? The cottage is locked and Adam's not home."

"Adam has gone to Kevin's for the weekend. Remind me to give you a key. Come in. I have lots to tell you. I came from the solicitor. John wants to reconcile."

"What! Are you serious?" Judy gave Katie a stern look. "You're not considering it... are you?"

"Absolutely not! Let's open a bottle of wine and I'll give you the scoop."

Judy lit a fire to take the evening chill off the morning room while Katie poured wine. They sipped on a nice Merlot while making dinner and talked of the inadequacies of ex-husbands. They even laughed about their shortcomings, of which there were many. Buddy curled up on his bed and Lily and Sam made a cozy golden hearth rug. Katie relished the comfortable scene and realized she had the life she wanted. Her past really was behind her.

Judy gave her a questioning smile. "How come you're not upset with John, the solicitor or your finances? In fact, you even look content."

"I am happy but I have to be realistic about money too.

Twelve hours a week, much less during the winter, at minimum wage and minimal rent from one tenant will not pay the bills. Any suggestions?"

They joined the dogs by the fire and curled up in the blue chairs. Judy hugged a yellow cushion. "Um, more hours at the bakery is out of the question. Who runs the gift shop?"

"Mrs. Barker and her daughter. She's been doing it for years. Nothing there."

"Okay. Let's evaluate your skills and what you enjoy doing. You enjoy caring for people, cooking and entertaining. Katie, this is a no brainer. Turn Lavender Cottage into a B&B."

"I don't know. Strangers in my house doesn't appeal. How do I get customers? Advertise or do that Airbnb thing?"

"Airbnb, now that's a perfect solution. Airbnb takes care of the advertising and bookings. You provide a comfortable room and breakfast, charge £50 or £60 a night."

"I don't know, the thought of complete strangers in my house. Airbnb doesn't check people out. They book with a credit card and that's it. They could be thieves or serial killers." Katie sipped her wine. "Am I being over cautious?"

"Just a bit, but if you're not comfortable, it wouldn't work for you."

"What if I did my own checking? I could look people up on Google or only take people who were referred to me from people I knew. If I didn't like them I could say I was booked up."

"A bit restrictive but it sounds as though you're warming up to the idea?"

Katie nodded. "The narrowboat owners would book for their friends. Bob knows most of the people so they wouldn't be complete strangers."

Fifteen

Bed and Breakfast

*K*atie and Judy talked late into the night, planning the Lavender Cottage B&B. They chose a sprig of purple lavender for the logo with the tagline 'Soothing and Relaxing' playing on the characteristics of lavender. Judy calculated that renting out three bedrooms on an average of two nights a week, together with Adam's rent, would equal an adequate income.

Katie's dining room furniture was set up in the large lounge. It was ideal for breakfast and the big fireplace and comfy chairs made it cozy. The front door led into the lounge by the stairs, a convenient place for a registration desk.

The morning room, Katie's favourite, the kitchen and a large pantry that she used as an office were saved as her private space.

Saturday morning found them, much later than usual, walking the dogs along the towpath when the red roof of Piers' narrowboat came into view and put-putted alongside them.

"Good morning, ladies," Piers called from *Tranquil Days* and Arthur barked his greeting to Buddy. Katie grabbed Buddy as he attempted to run up to the bridge, preparing to jump on board. Lily, the swimmer, who had been on her best behaviour, leaped into the water before Judy could restrain her, followed by Sam, seeing the opportunity for a swim.

"Lily! Sam!" Judy called, to no avail, as the dogs swam across the canal.

"Oh dear," Piers called. "I should know better. Retrievers can't wait to get into the water."

"My fault," Judy replied. "We usually walk in the fields but the dogs were behaving and Buddy likes the towpath. We took the risk."

Piers turned the engine off, allowing the boat to drift to the bank. Buddy saw his opportunity, wiggled out of Katie's arms, and jumped on board to greet Arthur.

"Come! Lily! Sam!" Judy called in her stern alpha voice and both dogs swam to the side. Two dripping wet retrievers climbed the muddy canal bank and shook their wet fur, soaking everyone with canal water. It caused the group to burst into laughter at the comical scene.

"Buddy can stay but not those two..." Piers said between laughs. "Why don't you come and visit later this afternoon, when Lily and Sam are clean and dry?" He smiled. "A nice bottle of Merlot is waiting." He winked at Katie. "Your favourite."

Katie took a breath to stop the blush rising from her neck and steady her voice, knowing that Judy was giving her a questioning scan. "We'd love to. Thanks."

Piers started the engine and steered the narrowboat toward the bridge with Buddy and Arthur sitting at the bow. Katie's cheeks were bright red. "Oh, I forgot Buddy." Seeing Piers always sparked something inside her and today he remembered her favourite wine. His glance into her eyes, brief at first, had lingered and she wondered if he sensed something too. *What is happening? Am I imagining something that is not there?* Piers waved as he steered the boat under the bridge, heading towards the marina.

"*K-a-t-i-e!* Is there something you're not telling me?"

"No. I often meet Piers when I'm walking Buddy and Bud loves to jump on the boat and sit with Arthur. That's all."

"I saw you blush like a school girl. You like him, don't you?"

"Piers is a nice guy but don't let your imagination run away with you. He's an excellent doctor. He was so good to Adam when he had his accident. While Adam recovered, he visited every day. I got to know him and he's kind and generous. A friend, nothing more."

"And your favourite wine?"

"Maybe I mentioned it." As they reached the canal basin, Katie saw Buddy on the dock. "Come, Buddy, time to go home," she called, relieved to change the subject.

Judy hosed Lily and Sam to get rid of the canal water, which was never clean and as the water warmed up in the summer, the odour would get worse. But it was still coolish and the hose-down rid the dogs of the canal smell but the wet dog aroma lingered. Ordered to sit in the sun by the rose garden, Lily and Sam put their heads on their front paws and slept.

Judy and Katie spent the afternoon working on a business plan, including a budget and marketing.

By the time they arrived at *Tranquil Days,* they had planned and organized the whole B&B project. Judy had typed it up on Katie's laptop with an introduction for Katie to hand around Bob's Marina. Opening day was scheduled for Whitsun Weekend, May 19th, only a month away.

"Hello, ladies, welcome to *Tranquil Days*." Piers held a hand out to help Katie into the boat, his warm touch tingling. She smiled at him. "Are we sitting outside today?"

"Yes. It's pleasant in the fresh air and the sun is warm. We could sit inside if you would prefer?"

"No, this is fine," Katie replied.

Piers had fitted seats around the stern, making it comfortable and pleasant for several people even if it wasn't as big as a cruising stern. A little metal table sat in the middle with cheese and crackers, a bowl of mixed nuts and three wine glasses full of Merlot.

Judy made a toast. "Cheers! Here's to Lavender Cottage B&B."

Piers smiled and raised his glass. "Tell me more?"

Katie jumped right in and babbled on about John's shocking news and how it had forced her to consider various options to earn money. Judy took over then and listed all the plans they had to open the B&B.

"Wow! That is a fabulous idea. You will be full all summer. Can I book a room for Whitsun Weekend? I'm entertaining friends." Katie saw the shadow again, not as intense, but it was there. "My anti-social behaviour has to change. Bob usually makes it special here at the marina to start off the season. I can only sleep four on the boat and if they are single, only two, so book me a room. Most of the boaters are in the same boat," he laughed. "Pardon the pun."

"My first booking. This is wild!" Katie thought she might

explode with excitement. "The winter might be stark though."

"No, winter will be busy," Piers said, "By October the boats are winterized, that is the water shut off and pipes drained. It's too cold to live on the boat without heat or water. A B&B would be a great option for boaters to come in the winter—a warm place to stay, food at Mary's or the pub while they check the boats or just enjoy a break."

Katie shivered as a cool breeze ruffled her hair and the sun dropped behind the trees. Piers put his hand on her shoulder. "Are you cold?"

"A little. It's time we left."

"We can go inside. It's heated." He smiled, his eyes bright.

"Thanks, but the dogs are hungry. It's their dinner time," Katie replied.

"Why don't we meet at the pub for dinner," Judy suggested. "We can spread the word about the B&B."

"That's a great idea. In an hour?" Piers asked Judy but glanced at Katie.

Sunday evening, Katie helped Judy load Lily and Sam in her truck. It wasn't a normal vehicle for a woman, but then Judy wasn't most women. Katie waved as the truck turned onto Main Street and then looked to Buddy. "Time for a walk?" He wagged his tail and trotted down Marina Lane towards the dock.

The setting sun emitted a red hue on the grey clouds, giving the sky a mottled texture, both pretty and ominous. Katie suspected the clouds meant rain or even a thunderstorm. The marina was quiet, the boaters having returned to the city. *Tranquil Days* was all closed up and Piers had mentioned he was on duty at the clinic most of the week. *Piers. What is it about that man? Is it his kindness? Gentleness?*Katie remembered how she had blushed. 'Like a schoolgirl,' Judy had said. Romance terrified her. She remembered how kind and considerate John was when they met and through most of the marriage. She never expected such a drastic change. Thinking of John was still painful and the deep hurt was hard to get over and she never planned to go through it again. Without warning, tears trickled down her cheeks and she vowed never to fall in love again—friendship and nothing more. Brushing her wet cheeks, she called out to Buddy. "Time to go home."

Judy had written out a list of all the things that needed to be done before opening the B&B. The furnishings needed updating. Melanie and Ben hadn't lived at home for years but Katie set the bedrooms up as though they still lived at home. Guilt tightened her diaphragm. Where would the kids stay when they came home? Well, she doubted Ben would be home soon. Melanie had her flat in Nottingham. *I can't plan my life around grown-up kids.*

She heard the front door close and Adam's voice came from the hall. "Anyone home?"

"I'm in the morning room. How was your weekend?"

Adam came into the room and claimed one of the blue chairs. "I had a good time. Kevin and I played darts at the pub on Saturday. Sonia sulked but Kevin told her off." Adam shrugged and gave a cheeky grin. "We drove out to a nice carvery for lunch today and even Sonia was pleasant. How was your weekend?"

"Good. Judy stayed for the weekend. She has an amazing idea, which might solve the financial issues. I need to talk to you as it will affect you and your living accommodation."

Adam's face turned white, he took a deep breath and hesitated before speaking. "Do you want me to move out? Please, Katie. I love living here."

"No, Adam, no! Your home will always be here." Katie explained the plans for a B&B and showed him the work that she and Judy had done over the weekend.

"I am not asking you to move out but I am asking you to give up one of your rooms. We would make you a bed-sitting room. We'll share the kitchen and morning room, leaving the lounge for the guests. Pretty much as we do now."

"One room is all I need. How can I help?"

"I'm nervous about opening my home to strangers so it'll be safer with the two of us. We'll make a good team."

The next morning, Katie walked up to Cyril's antique store to see what he had to furnish the bedrooms. She wanted the rooms to be authentic and rustic.

"Good morning, Katie, I'm assuming you are shopping for furniture for your B&B?"

Katie's eyes widened. "How did you know?"

"Word travels fast in a village. Maisie told me at the pub. It's a great idea. I will book out-of-town clients attending auctions. When are you opening?"

"Whitsun Weekend."

"Would you consider opening the week before? My next big auction is May 15th? I'd book three rooms."

Katie shrugged, not sure what to say. "I don't see why not. I'd better get some furniture, though. Cyril, I'm on a budget and these antiques are expensive. I like the best but I can't afford it."

Cyril was a good salesman and persuaded Katie to take three antique wardrobes, three chests of drawers and three headboards. A sideboard for the dining room, a dinner trolley, a variety of silver servers and a few ornaments.

At the end, he guided her across the room to a Victorian style three-piece suite. "For you! It's perfect for your lounge."

"I don't need a suite. I bought the blue chairs for the morning room and returned the mushroom ones to the lounge." Katie frowned. "Oh, it's the beige, isn't it? Sorry the beige stays."

Cyril sighed. "All right, maybe later." He handed her the bill. Katie swallowed hard. "Well, as nice as all this is, I can't afford it. Let's back up and consider alternatives."

"If my name is on the furniture, it has to be the best."

"Cyril, you are not paying the bill. This is about double my budget," Katie said. "Here's an idea. What if I displayed a sign in the bedrooms and lounge? Furniture supplied by Springsville Antique Shop. For more details contact Cyril Winthrop"

"I like that idea but only if you buy the best. I don't want to advertise junk. Not that I stock any junk," he added, with haste.

"Well, that will depend on you. In return for the advertising, you could either loan me the furniture or sell it for a discounted price I can afford."

It took most of the morning but Katie and Cyril struck a bargain by reducing the price on some items and loaning others.

Katie almost skipped down Main Street, pleased with her choices and bargaining skills. She had three rooms booked, opening a week early. She stopped skipping as panic hit her stomach. "What was I thinking? How can I be ready in three weeks?"

Sixteen

Katie in her Element

*F*ear pinched Katie's stomach as she heard Cyril's voice declaring the wonders of Springsville. She couldn't help breaking into a smile as he over-pronounced his words, marbles filling his mouth. *Why do you do that, Cyril?* His county accent was naturally cultured, but she acknowledged his need to impress.

Katie opened the front door. "Good afternoon. Welcome to Lavender Cottage. Please, come in." All nervousness gone, Katie greeted an older gentleman, not much taller than she. His tweed jacket was undone and she doubted it would close over his rounded belly. Katie grinned, his stature reminding her of Santa Claus.

"Ms. Saunders, may I introduce Sir Walter Rutherford? He is attending the auction tomorrow."

Sir Walter, Katie thought swallowing hard. *Definitely not Santa.* "Sir Walter, I hope you'll be comfortable. The B&B is not the Dorchester by any stretch of the imagination and I must confess that you are my first guest."

Cyril was backing out of the door. "I shall leave you in the capable hands of Ms. Saunders. Tomorrow's viewing begins at 9 a.m. and the auction at 11. Enjoy your evening."

Sir Walter turned his attention to Katie. "Ms. Saunders, Cyril likes to use my title. I don't. It's an honour bestowed on me without merit. This accommodation suits me far better than The Dorchester." His soft round face broke into a warm kind smile. Katie liked him for it. "I am honoured to be your first guest."

"Please, call me Katie." She took a seat behind the desk and registered Sir Walter, handing him keys. She pointed to the antique sideboard. "Help yourself to tea, coffee and biscuits or cake. This is the guest lounge. If it cools off in the evening, Adam will light a fire. Breakfast is between 7 and 10 a.m. Tea and coffee will be available from 6." She glanced at the Keurig machine. It wasn't her choice but the easiest way to have fresh coffee all day. She doubted Sir Walter would know how to use it though. "If you need help with the machine or have questions, please knock on my door." She motioned towards the morning room.

She led the way upstairs and opened the bedroom door, allowing Sir Walter to step inside. "What a delightful room. Cyril has supplied you with lovely antiques. That wardrobe is a magnificent piece of Regency, quite rare."

"Cyril likes the best and I love antique furniture. I confess I choose things by my preference, rather than knowledge."

"And that, my dear, is how it should be."

"I'll leave you to get settled."

"Ah, this is perfect." Sir Walter stood by the window, staring at the garden. He appeared pensive; not sad or troubled but thoughtful.

"Please stroll in the garden or relax on the patio or porch. You may bump into Adam. He lives here and tends the garden."

Sir Walter answered without taking his eyes off the garden. "I will, thank you." Katie left, closing the door.

Four more guests arrived for the auction. There was a young couple, antique collectors from Manchester, and two dealers from London who had agreed to share the room with twin beds. Almost a full house. It was good practice for the official opening on Friday.

The alarm jangled in Katie's ear at 5 a.m. It was getting light but dark grey clouds covered any sign of sun. Rain droplets slid down the window but, despite the grey, she leaped out of bed, happy and eager to please her guests. Buddy patted downstairs in front of her only to stop and stare, wondering why they were up at dawn. Adam joined them but neither spoke. Katie giggled quietly, feeling like a kid creeping out of the house after bedtime. Not wanting to disturb the guests, they remained silent until they closed the morning room door.

"Good morning, Adam. You're up early." Katie said, opening the back door for Buddy, who looked at the rain and went back to curl up on his bed.

"You make the breakfast and I'll light the fires. I think the guests will appreciate a fire in the guest lounge this morning. It will take the chill and dampness out of the air."

"Excellent idea."

Katie carried a tray of dishes and condiments to the dining room table just as Sir Walter stepped off the last stair, wrapped in a tartan dressing gown. First he stared at the Keurig machine and then at it Katie. She smiled. *I was right about Sir Walter.*

"Good morning, Sir Walter. Can I help?"

"I'd like a cup of tea but these fandangle machines are a mystery."

"Why don't you go back upstairs and I'll have Adam bring you a morning tea. What do you like in it?" As she said the words, Katie decided she should offer a morning tea service. Lots of people liked their first cup of tea or coffee in bed.

"Thank you, that would be nice. Strong with a little milk, please."

The auction guests appeared at the breakfast table at about the same time. Katie was pleased she'd had the foresight to prepare the bacon and sausage ahead of time, leaving the toast and eggs until the last minute. Adam was a great help and she realized breakfast for a full house would take two people.

The guests chatted around the table, enjoying the crackling fire and lingering with their second cup of tea or coffee. At ten to nine, in a flurry of conversation and excitement, they left. Katie cleared the table, surprised to find Sir Walter tucked in the beige easy chair, sipping on tea in front of the fire.

"You're not going to the preview?"

"No, I previewed yesterday. This is lovely, Ms. Saunders." He hesitated. "Katie, I wonder if I could stay on a few nights."

"Of course. How many nights? I am booked at the weekend."

"Two more. I'll check out on Friday morning but I need rest. This is a perfect place. You don't offer meals other than breakfast, do you?"

"No, but Mary's Bakery and Café makes super sandwiches and baked goods for lunches and light meals. And the Boaters Inn serves evening meals."

"Thank you. I'll finish my tea and then get to the auction. I'll see you later." Katie felt dismissed. Whatever was troubling Sir Walter, he needed to be alone. She wondered if he was recovering from or struggling with an illness. Intuition told Katie that he needed some kind of care.

The morning room door opened and Adam said, "Sorry to interrupt."

"That's okay," Katie said, heading to the morning room. She closed the door with a last glance at Sir Walter.

"It's stopped raining so I'm off to work in the garden. I want to get the patio set up for guests."

"Let's hope the rain stays off and we have a nice weekend. By the way, Sir Walter is staying two more nights. He likes the garden and I sense he might appreciate talking to someone. He seems lost. If it's appropriate, strike up a conversation."

"I felt lost after Doris died. Perhaps he's a widower."

"Maybe. Or he needs rest. We'll make his stay restful and hopefully he enjoys the garden."

Grateful for a dry, breezy day, Katie washed the linens and hung them outside to dry. She had an electric clothes dryer but preferred fresh air. She'd have no choice but to use the dryer when they were busy.

Katie sniffed the fresh linen as she entered through the porch, Doris' chair rocking in unison with Adam. She left them to their private conversation. He was a hard worker but at 75, Adam needed frequent breaks from the heavy garden work. Doris was a good distraction but it wasn't enough; she needed to hire a younger man to do the digging. The phone rang and she ran into the house.

"Melanie, how lovely to hear from you. Where are you?"

"I'm stranded at Lima Airport. Cancelled flight. I'm on

standby for the next one. I can't get hold of Phil. He planned to meet me at East Midlands. Can you let him know? I'll text as soon as I land at Heathrow."

"Of course. Are you okay? I wasn't expecting you for another month."

"I'm fine. The university wrapped everything up sooner than we expected. Some of the team stayed, but I wanted to come back."

"You sound disappointed."

"I'm disappointed they cancelled the program. I loved the work but I'm looking forward to getting home."

"Do you need a bed?" Katie hesitated. Melanie no longer had a bed at home and she felt guilty. "I've opened the B&B and we're booked. You could bunk with me."

"No, Mum, I'll stay at Phil's. I get my apartment back at the end of the month."

"Oh, I see." Katie was disappointed. She loved having her daughter around. She wondered about Phil but didn't like to ask if the stay was a relationship or helping a friend.

"I'll call you as soon as I can, and I'll drop in Saturday or Sunday. I must go. This roaming is costing me a fortune. Love you."

"Love you too," Katie said as the line clicked and the dial tone buzzed in her ear. She replaced the receiver, sensing disloyalty, as though she was kicking her daughter out. She had maintained Melanie and Ben's bedrooms so they could always come home but now she didn't have room for them. Buddy sat at her feet. He always knew when things were not quite right. "Okay, Bud, let's go for a walk and clear my head."

Buddy bounded to the marina where they found Bob, hammer in hand, as he repaired the dock. The air had a faint smell of oil paint from touching up the boats and loud quacking came from a bunch of mallards. Mums and dads with a trail of little ones were quacking for human treats; sparse with no boaters around. In two days' time the place would be full of boaters telling winter tales and making summer plans. Piers had booked a double room for friends from Nottingham and Katie assumed he had guests on the boat too. Bob had booked the other two rooms for boaters from the marina.

Buddy ran ahead, stopping at the stile. If Sam and Lily were with them, they would walk back through the fields but, today, Katie sat on the wooden step of the stile. She felt happy and grateful to be taking care of people again, not just family. Making people's lives pleasant and comfortable was what she excelled at. Once again, the sense of guilt hit her. Was she abandoning her children for strangers? On an intellectual level, Katie knew the children no longer needed their mum. Melanie had made other plans, not even expecting to stay at home. Her bedroom was in another place and Ben had found his home in New York. "The kids have moved on and I must too." Buddy sat at her feet, his underbelly muddy from the morning rain. His head cocked to one side, she admired his muzzle, dirty from sniffing the muddy ground. "That's a look of agreement, my friend. It's just you and me now, Bud. We'll do a good job of taking care of strangers and making their day a little nicer. We'd better get back though and give you a bath."

Katie opened the back gate and yelled. "Adam, don't let Buddy in the house. He's muddy. I need…" She stopped at the porch, seeing Sir Walter sitting in Doris' rocking chair. It had never occurred to her that offering the porch to guests also meant offering Doris' chair. She glanced at Adam who smiled, his eyes saying it was okay.

"Sir Walter, you've met Adam. How did the auction go?"

"I think Cyril made a lot of money. Adam has shown me around his wonderful garden."

"Excellent. Who would like a cup of tea?" Adam nodded and Sir Walter hesitated. "I'll make a pot of fresh tea, not the machine stuff."

"In that case, I would love a cup of tea. And Katie, could I ask you to drop the "Sir"? Walter suits me much better."

"Walter, of course. Fresh tea is coming up." They laughed and Katie picked up Buddy, holding him in the air as she walked into the kitchen. She dried him off with his big doggie towel. "That'll do for now. I'll bathe you later."

After carrying the tray of tea to the porch, she left the men to talk. She needed to call Phil. He had already received Melanie's message and told Katie that she was on a flight home.

Sir Walter drove away after breakfast on Friday morning, assuring Katie that he had had a wonderful time and would be back. He appeared more relaxed but he was still a mystery. She wondered if he had talked to Adam but with new guests arriving within the hour, she had no time to ask. Perhaps it was a guy thing and Adam wouldn't reveal any secrets. Her mind was racing with possibilities when a familiar voice called. "Hello! It's me, Mum!"

Katie ran down stairs and threw her arms around Melanie. "I'm thrilled to see you but I am so busy today."

"I know. The official opening. I'm here to help. It's exciting and I want to be part of it. I don't start class until next week, so here I am. Put me to work."

Tears tightened Katie's throat. She had been thinking of her worries about Melanie and now here she was, ready to roll up her sleeves. "I am so glad you are here. I'm stripping the bed. A guest just left and the other rooms are ready. Can you make sure there's tea and coffee for the machine and tidy up the guest lounge? Maybe vacuum it too?"

"No problem. Oh, you've got a Keurig machine. I love these and your guests will enjoy having twenty-four-hour tea and coffee."

"Some do, some don't. It's good for coffee but my generation prefers tea in a pot."

"I get it. Mum, the purist." Melanie shook her head and smiled. "I'm proud of you, Mum. You have blossomed since you moved here. Are you happy?"

"Yes. I enjoy taking care of people and adding sparkle to their lives. The B&B lets me do that."

"I dropped in to visit Dad yesterday. He's come down in the world and become rather pathetic. I should warn you; he's talking about you two getting back together."

"I know. I had a letter from the solicitor. I don't want him back and I gave up the alimony. He has no ties anymore and that suits me fine." Katie glanced at Melanie. "I'm sorry. I know he's your father but I've moved on."

"I'll keep in touch but I lost all respect for him when he abandoned you for that floozie. He's reaping the rewards, or more like consequences, and it looks good on him."

Katie and Melanie worked all morning preparing extra treats. Adam stayed in the garden and arranged the patio with tables and large sun umbrellas. He even cut flowers for the guest rooms.

"I think we are done," Katie said, placing a vase full of spring flowers on the sideboard and giving the lounge one last satisfied look. "I'll make lunch and we can sit on the patio. I want you to tell me all about your plans."

"Not much to tell. I'll be back in the lecture hall on Monday, until the end of the semester. I have students lining up to work with me. Most are curious but there are some promising summer students and I have reports to do from the Peru project. That will take me a few weeks."

"How are things at Phil's?"

"Fine. It's strange living on our old street. Everyone asks after you. I'll be happy to get my flat back."

"And?"

"Mum! I like Phil and he likes me but neither of us wants to commit. Oh, I almost forgot. Phil starts work at the university in September and he's working on an environmental project with them this summer."

"I think you inspired him. Phil was a good friend in my darkest days." Katie laughed. "That seems like a lifetime ago."

Seventeen

Problems with Men

Once the guests had settled, Katie assured Melanie that she was okay on her own. She loved having her daughter around, but the frequent glances at the clock and the glow on her cheeks told her Melanie was eager to meet Phil for dinner. Katie smiled, convinced that her daughter had found her mate in Phil. They just didn't know it yet.

Piers had invited Katie to join his guests on board for a cocktail, followed by dinner at the Boater's Inn. Cindy and Rick were the guests at Lavender Cottage. Rick, a doctor at the clinic, worked with Piers, and his wife Cindy enjoyed being a stay-at-home mum. When Katie told her she chose to stay home with the kids, it was an immediate friendship. Together, they walked to *Tranquil Days*. Cindy leaned into Katie, whispering. "How can they cram one more person in the stern?"

"Well, I guess we're about to find out." The two giggled as

they were helped into the cramped space. Piers introduced Katie to a young couple whose names Katie didn't remember. The words that reached her ears were: my sister-in-law. *Did that mean Piers was a married man? Why should that bother me?* she thought. A flamboyant and loud woman, both in voice and dress, interrupted her over-active thoughts.

"I'm Debra. Piers and I go back a long way." She turned to Piers. "Don't we, darling?" He either wasn't listening or chose to ignore her as he continued his conversation with Rick. Debra's presence, alone, filled the cramped narrowboat.

The men sat up on the deck, leaving the seats for the women but Debra squeezed in between Piers and Rick. Katie tried to ignore the sight of her hand patting Piers' thigh. The woman laughed a lot, often when things weren't funny. It appeared to be an odd relationship. Piers had never mentioned her but then he hadn't mentioned a sister-in-law either. On reflection, she knew little about him. She'd only discovered he was a doctor by accident.

Rick jumped down and sat by Cindy, whispering in her ear. She nodded, looking straight at Debra. Piers reached for the wine and his long legs touched the floor with ease as he slid off the cabin roof. Wine bottle in hand, he topped up everyone's glass. His eyes moved from the wine to Katie. He didn't notice the wine droplets spill on the side of her glass. His warm grin broadened and something stirred inside her.

"You're spilling the wine."

"Oops! Sorry. Did it spill on you?"

She shook her head and wiped the glass with a napkin. Speaking was out of the question, resulting in an awkward silence. Katie looked at the other guests. No one had noticed, except Debra.

Piers took a breath. "I'm hearing wonderful reports about the B&B. My guess is you'll be full all summer." He patted her on the shoulder and she tried to ignore the warm tingle, shaking it off. Piers must have seen it because he gave her a strange look. "You worked hard and you deserve a break." Piers turned to Rick. "Any comments, Rick?"

"It's perfect. We even had tea and biscuits in bed this morning. That's more than I get at home," he said, playfully pulling Cindy close to him. Cindy laughed, punching his arm.

Piers was still standing in front of Katie and another awkward moment ensued. He bent down to pet Buddy, curled at her feet, and Arthur toddled over to join them.

"You are coming to Boater's Inn for dinner…" He turned sharply as Debra bent over his back. Her chin was on his shoulder as she tried to whisper something in his ear. Piers pushed her away. "What are you doing? Don't whisper. It's rude."

Debra jumped back and pouted. "Oh, nothing."

Katie fidgeted in her seat, uncomfortable with the scene. Debra was throwing herself at Piers and it appeared that the attention was unwanted.

"I'm sorry. My plans have changed. In fact, I had better get back to Lavender Cottage."

Piers frowned, his eyes pleading. Now Katie was uncomfortable and confused. "Are you sure? I thought you said you would join us."

Katie shook her head and climbed over the side of the boat to the dock, calling out to Buddy. "Lovely to meet you all. Have a good evening." She looked at Piers' disappointed face and at Debra's triumphant smile. Questions flew through her mind. Was she overreacting? Why would Piers invite her, unless they were a couple? Debra was staying on the boat so where was she sleeping? Memories of John's infidelity and deceit jabbed at her heart. What about the sister-in-law?It made little sense and Katie told herself she was happy to be out of it, if confused.Was she jealous?As she and Buddy walked back to the cottage, she gave herself a pep talk. "Don't be ridiculous. Jealous of what?" The words had burst out of her mouth louder than she intended.

As she approached the cottage, she saw an old Vauxhall parked by the front gate. Katie frowned, wondering who was visiting. Buddy's tail wagged with caution at first but as the occupant climbed out of the car, his tail whipped back and forth and he ran to the car. Katie panicked. Her heart pounded in her ears. It was John.

"What the hell does he want?" she whispered.

"Hello!" John called, his jacket hanging forward as he bent down to pet Buddy. He looked scrawny. "How are you? The place looks nice."

"What are you doing here?" Katie's tone snapped. She had an urge to slap his pasty white face. He was intruding on her world.

"I'm visiting my wife."

"Your ex-wife. We are no longer married."

"Technically, yes. Can we talk?"

Katie's inside boiled like a witch's cauldron, anger bubbling to the surface. She glanced at the skinny pathetic man and wondered how she had ever loved him. "Come down in the world, I see," she said with a glance at the old car.

"I lost everything, Katie. Even the partners ganged up against me and…"

Katie interrupted. "I don't care about your problems and

153

there is nothing to talk about. Please leave."

"Katie p-l-e-a-s-e! I only want to talk." He nodded to a passerby. "Somewhere private. I know I made a terrible mistake."

"I don't want to talk. You are not coming in the house." Katie saw Adam working in the garden and watching them, his stare intense.

John's face darkened, with hurt or anger, it was hard to tell. "If you won't invite me in, then can we go to the pub?"

Katie thought for a moment. The pub was preferable to the cottage. She didn't want him tainting her lovely home. At the pub, they would not be alone. She brushed away the hackles standing at attention on the back of her neck. Something about him had triggered a primal fear. John had changed and not for the better.

"Okay. We can go to the Boater's Inn. I can't be long as I have guests at the B&B this weekend."

It was early for the evening crowd at the pub and Katie pointed to a quiet table in the corner. John pulled on his trouser pocket, his face scarlet. "I don't have enough money to buy drinks."

She grinned as she walked to the bar, knowing how humiliating it was for John to admit he had no money. She ordered a lager and lime and a pint of best bitter. A flash memory of happier times came back to her, times long past.

"I assume you still drink beer?" she said placing the drinks on the table. "Now, talk."

"Katie, I'm very sorry about how I treated you. I'm sorry for being unfaithful and for all the pain I caused you."

Katie was stunned by the words of apology that she had longed to hear. But now spoken, they were meaningless.

"I'm over it and I've moved on. I appreciate your effort but it's too little, too late."

"I want to get back together, try again. Maybe get married. Wouldn't that be fun?"

"Are you out of your mind?" Katie yelled.

"Shush, not so loud. I'm serious. I am sorry. How many times do I have to say it? Everyone makes mistakes."

"You threw thirty-three years of marriage down the drain just to have a fling and find your youth, which is long gone. You spent all our savings on a fancy condo, women and cars. Those are big mistakes. I doubt I can ever forgive you."

"Please, Katie. I have nothing. You have a cottage and a business. I'm willing to help with the B&B. The old fellow can't be much help."

Her blood was boiling. How dare John walk into her life and expect to take over? "Don't you dare insult Adam; he works hard. The B&B is mine. I didn't squander my share of the money; I put it to work. The judge made it abundantly clear that once I gave up the alimony, neither of us had a claim on the other. You are on your own, John."

"You don't understand. The partners fired me. I don't have a job. They said I wasn't pulling my weight, which wasn't true. I messed up a couple of cases but I didn't deserve to get fired."

"That is not my problem. Find another job."

Katie sensed that someone was staring and she turned toward the door to see Piers looking at her. He looked puzzled and raised an eyebrow. She wanted to say 'this isn't what it looks like.' She wanted to explain and then she saw Debra hanging off his arm. Cindy and Rick followed, saying hello. Katie acknowledged their greeting and watched the group move towards a large reserved table set up for dinner. She even noticed a spare chair, the one she should have been sitting in instead of arguing with John.

John saw the looks. "Friends of yours?"

"Guests at the B&B. Not that it's any of your business." Katie wanted to crawl under the table, out of sight, and disown John.

"They look cozy-friendly to me." John's tone was sarcastic.

"Like I said, none of your business. John, finish your beer. It's time you left." John stayed sitting as Katie moved towards the door. "Katie, I have nowhere to go. I am two months behind on the rent and the landlord won't wait. Unless I give him £400 today, I'm on the street."

"Well, I guess you are on the street."

John stood up and grabbed her arm, pulling her off balance. He shrugged his shoulders and laughed towards Piers table. "Too much to drink."

As soon as they were on the street, Katie slapped him across the face. "Don't you ever say that again in front of my friends."

He grabbed her arm again, his nails digging into her flesh. Fear gripped her stomach. John was a different person. His agitation moved from anger to rage. Something was wrong and for the second time that night, she feared him. Her impulse was to run back into the pub.

She riffled through her handbag and pulled a wad of pound notes from her purse. "Here, take this. It's all I have. Pay your landlord and get out of my life. Now leave!" He snatched the money from her hand.

Adam's voice called, "Is everything all right, Katie?"

"Mind your own business, old man."

"Katie is my business," Adam retorted glaring at John.

John gave a nasty laugh. "Cradle snatcher. She's half your age, old man. Oh, that is funny, Katie," John scoffed and cackled.

"All you can get is an old man."

"John, what has gotten in to you?" Katie's face creased with worry. She had never seen him like this. He was sweating and his eyes were darting from one place to another. "Are you ill?"

"I'm fine." He pushed by Adam and walked down Main Street, shoving the money in his pocket.

"Who is he? Why did you give him money? Did he steal it?"

"John is my ex-husband. He's seen better times." Katie was close to tears. Her heart was pounding and she was scared for her own safety and for John. "I've never seen him behave like that." She gave Adam a quizzical look. "What are you doing here?"

"I didn't like the way he was talking to you earlier and thought I'd make sure you were okay." Adam grinned. "I've never been called a cradle snatcher. Doris will get a laugh out of that. Come on, let me take you home."

Katie leaned on his shoulder and pecked his cheek. "Thank you for rescuing me." Adam reminded her of her father, who had died of cancer ten years ago. She wondered if that was why she had taken Adam under her wing. It hadn't occurred to her before today.

They walked across the village green and entered by the back gate. The sweet fragrance of the last of the lilac filled the evening air as the evening primroses opened their petals. Katie appreciated the warmth and gentle calm of home. When they reached the porch, Doris was rocking, and they sat down to join her. Katie had added two more rocking chairs for guests. Doris didn't mind the guests enjoying the porch, as long as she and Adam had their quiet moments.

Doris' voice was always a whisper on the wind. Even on the calm nights, the porch had a breeze. *'You're upset, Katie. That*

157

man is no good. Stay away from him.'

"There is something wrong with him. In thirty-three years of marriage, John never lifted a finger or said a cross word."

'Whatever is wrong, John is in big trouble and you can't help him. He will destroy you. Stay away. Adam, talk sense into her. Doris' voice was fading as the breeze stilled. *We'll talk tomorrow Adam...'*

Adam stared at Katie. "Why did you give him money? That may have been a mistake."

"To be honest, a part of me pities him. He can't pay his rent and I don't want him in this cottage. John asked that we get together again. He even suggested marriage." Katie laughed. "As if that would ever happen."

Adam gave her a thoughtful look. "I know you, Katie, and so does John. He knows you are compassionate and thinks he can win you over, given time. You must be strong. How much money did you give him?

"£400. The money I had taken out of the bank today to pay for the gardening and supplies for the week. Everything I made from my guests this weekend."

"Katie, you can't keep handing him money. He'll be back for more. Promise me you'll call the police if he comes back. I don't trust him."

"That's harsh. For all his faults, he's never been threatening or abusive. He's just not himself right now," Katie said and frowned as the front door banged shut. "What was that?" Panic gripped her throat. *Has John come back? That's silly. He doesn't have a key.*

"Your guests are returning," Adam said.

"Ah, yes. It'll take getting used to, having people come and go."

John's visit had thrown Katie off kilter. She tried not to think about it but his words kept creeping into her thoughts. She busied herself with the B&B guests and tried to ignore their friendship with Piers. His coolness had not gone unnoticed. She wanted to explain why she'd been in the pub with John but Piers had barely said hello. He was avoiding her.

On the whole, the weekend had gone well at Lavender Cottage. The guests praised Katie's hospitality and Rick and Cindy had booked another weekend in June. Even John's behaviour didn't detract from Katie's sense of accomplishment. She smiled, happy and content. The B&B business was her calling.

Eighteen

Changes

~∞~

Monday mornings at the marina were always quiet. The boaters had returned to their city jobs and the narrowboats sat still, waiting for the next weekend.

Katie walked to the dock with Buddy and glanced at *Tranquil Days*, hoping to see Piers. Buddy gave a little whimper and looked up. She patted his head. "Sorry, Bud. Arthur went back to the city. No playing today." She waved at Bob, who was checking the fuel levels on the petrol pumps.

"Good morning, Katie. How'd the weekend go at the B&B?"

Katie gave him a 'thumbs up' before tying Buddy to the dog moorings at Mary's café.

"Morning, Mary, a large coffee to go, please."

"Coming up!" Mary's eyes hovered over Katie. "Is everything okay?"

"Yes. I'm just tired."

"I heard you had an unwanted visitor."

"Word travels fast around here. My ex-husband turned up." Katie's eyes moistened and a strange panic gripped her throat. "John's in bad shape. I'd rather not talk about it."

"Here's your coffee. I'm always here if you need a friend."

Katie nodded and picked up her coffee. "Thanks. A long walk in the fresh air will clear my head. Bye!"

Buddy woofed as Katie unhooked the leash and let him run along the towpath. She smiled, breathing in the fresh air as her mood changed to contentment. Happier than she had ever felt in her adult life, except for when her children were born. What had she done to deserve such happiness? Was she deserving? Katie's self-doubt returned, caused by John. She stood still in the middle of the towpath. "John," she said. She recalled his worrisome behaviour, aware that the change was dramatic, even sudden. Neither of them were the same as on their wedding day but basic personalities didn't change. John had his faults and midlife had hit him hard. She grinned. He could be stupid and never thought things through, which explained the fast cars and trophy girlfriends. But the aggression and abuse was not John. Something was wrong and she couldn't ignore it. As she walked back to the cottage, the question was, what could she do about it?

Adam called from the rose garden. "The phone's been ringing all morning. I was too dirty to go inside so I let the answering machine take the calls."

"Okay!"

Katie tapped the button to listen to the calls. The first two message were hang-ups but the machine had caught background noise. Both were identical, peculiar sounds. Jerky breathing as though someone had hiccups. An icy chill shot down her spine. She wrapped her arms around herself, frowned and hit the save button twice, noting four messages, all inquiring about the B&B.

By lunchtime, Katie had returned all the calls, made several bookings and prepared lunch for Adam. Excited about the new guests, Katie joined him in the rose garden, placing sandwiches and coffee on the patio table.

"Did the phone calls result in bookings?" Adam asked.

"Yes. Booked for the next two weekends and one family has booked two rooms for a whole week at the end of July. The last call will make you happy. Sir Walter is arriving tomorrow for three days. You enjoyed his company last time."

"Sir Walter is a nice man and enjoys the garden. He's quite an expert on roses. Is Cyril having another auction?"

"I assume so. I only spoke with Sir Walter's secretary." Katie hesitated. "Adam, there are some strange messages. Well, they're not messages, just a peculiar noise on the answering machine. It sounds creepy. Would you take a listen?"

"Of course. Most likely a wrong number. I'll do it after lunch." They ate lunch and relaxed in the sun.

"I'll go take a listen to those messages." Adam slipped off his muddy boots and walked through the French doors into the morning room. Katie followed.

Adam pushed the button on the answering machine and listened. "Like I said, a wrong number. I noticed street sounds so someone walking with a mobile; pocket calls, no doubt. I'm not sure why they would call twice but I'll delete them." Adam frowned. "What is it? You look worried."

"I found it creepy but your explanation would account for the weird noise." The phone rang. "No peace for the wicked," Katie laughed, leaning into the morning room for the cordless phone. She listened, shivered and glanced at Adam.

"Hello? Who are you? I know someone is there." She handed the phone to Adam.

Adam pressed it to his ear. "Identify yourself! If this is a joke, it's not funny." He shrugged and hung up. "It's nothing. A wrong number or kids fooling around."

"I guess so," she replied. She wasn't convinced because whoever was on the other end gave her chills. The phone rang again and Katie jumped off her seat, spilling coffee. Adam answered while she mopped up.

"Hello... Yes, your mum's right here. Just a moment."

Katie took a deep breath, relieved it was her daughter. The anxiety returned when she heard Melanie's voice.

"Melanie, what's wrong? You sound upset." She looked at Adam, her face grim with worry as she listened to her daughter. Slowly replacing the receiver, she turned to Adam. "That was Melanie. John turned up at her flat last night, hammering on the door. She wasn't home so knew nothing about it. Her landlady, who lives on the ground floor, called the police. They arrested John for drunk and disorderly. Phil drove to the police station and talked to the police. They suggested John needed help and gave Phil the number for the addiction centre. I guess he needs to dry out. I don't understand. John was never a big drinker."

"Where is he now?"

"Phil took him home. The police didn't charge him. But, here's the funny thing. John's landlord asked Phil for the rent. He gave the landlord a cheque for two months. What did John do with the money I gave him?"

"Sounds as though he drank it."

"I doubt it. He always got sick to his stomach if he drank liquor and three or four beers were his maximum."

"People turn to alcohol to ease their pain. One or two are never enough. John was aggressive on Saturday. That could be the drink. You said he'd changed."

Deep in thought, Katie ignored Adam's comment. "Maybe I should go to him."

"That's not a good idea. He might hurt you. Let Melanie and Phil sort it out."

"Perhaps you're right. Melanie said to wait. She's trying to get an appointment at the addiction centre. Phil and John were, are, friends from our years on Autumn Road. Phil's a good guy. He'll help if he can."

"It's better if you leave this to Melanie and Phil."

Katie nodded. She didn't want to confront John, afraid of him now. With her last thought, the chills returned and she realized the breathy phone calls were probably John.

Melanie had willingly taken on the role of dealing with him, making Katie uncomfortable. But she trusted Phil. He would protect her daughter and perhaps it was the best solution.

Katie, always the worrier, was on high alert but unsure of the reasons. John's behaviour was so out of character that she wondered if he might be losing his mind. Was it her sense of guilt for not wanting John here? He was a different man, and she had no feelings of love. At best, it was pity. They were odd emotions for Katie. A more practical, less emotional, woman was emerging and it frightened her. Was she changing too much? Would she become cold and calculating?

During the next two days, Katie's heart pounded as though she was teetering on the edge of a precipice. John had refused to go to the addiction centre. When Phil tried to force him,

John had punched him and told Melanie to get out of his life.

The first ring of the phone made Katie jump. John's pleading voice on the other end was pushing her to the edge. But she stood her ground, warning him that if he turned up, she'd call the police. Her actions were not her own; she sounded harsh and unfeeling. She couldn't even bring herself to talk to Adam. Riddled with guilt and wrestling with unfamiliar feelings, she retired early and fell into an exhausted sleep.

Katie's eyes shot open. The noise was deafening and the house was shaking. She lay on her back, trying to understand what was happening. Adam's bedroom door opened and the hall light shone under her door. Footsteps bounded downstairs. Instinct told her that John was hammering on the door.

Adam called out "Who is it?"

The banging stopped but no one replied.

Katie stood halfway down the stairs, mouthing the word 'John.' Adam nodded and put his finger to his mouth.

"Who's there?" Adam asked again.

A muffled voice said. "John. I want Katie."

"She's sleeping. Come back in the morning." Adam jumped back from the door as it vibrated with a loud thud.

"NO! NOW!"

"Okay, okay," Adam called. "Wait there. I'll go get her." Katie raised her eyebrows at Adam as he walked up the stairs towards her. Then she saw the phone in his hand, the display window emitting light. Adam had called emergency services. "They're on their way," he whispered.

The banging started again and Adam yelled. "She's getting dressed. Stop banging."

Blue lights finally flashed from behind the curtains. The

police had arrived. "Come with me, sir," a loud, assertive voice boomed.

Adam stood at the door and they listened to a scuffle followed by footsteps walking away. He unlocked the door and ushered in a second police officer. Katie stared through the open door as the policeman put his hand on John's head and eased him into the back of the squad car. Tears filled Katie's eyes. *How could it have come to this?*

Sir Walter stood at her side. "Come, my dear. The police will want to take statements." His voice was like magic, smooth and reassuring.

"Sir Walter, I'm so sorry about all this. I'm afraid I had forgotten you were here."

"Don't worry. I'm glad I was. That man is dangerous." He took her hand and led her into the morning room where Adam had taken the policeman.

The officer took statements and praised Adam for his quick reaction. The headlights from a taxi had woken him. Recognized John as the passenger and expecting trouble, he'd dialed 999, leaving the line open. The dispatcher listened and recorded the whole incident. John would be charged.

Gossip and scandal flooded Springsville the next day. Flashing police cars in the middle of the night made an exciting event but not exciting enough for the locals. Katie heard many stories, from gun brandishing youths stealing her jewels to a vengeful jealous lover.

On Friday morning, every table in Mary's café was occupied and the noise of animated chatter was deafening. Katie set the record straight. She yelled over the hub, relating the true story to Mary and knowing the crowd would listen. Audible sighs came from the tables. Katie and Mary laughed. An ex-husband wanting shelter was not as exciting as the local speculations. Katie sipped on her coffee and waved goodbye to Mary as she freed Buddy from the dog mooring for a run down the towpath. She was raw inside. The vision of John in the police car haunted her and she hoped the fresh morning breeze would blow it away. Buddy barked and the familiar putt-putt of a narrowboat drew closer. Her heart flipped into her throat as *Tranquil Days* approached the bridge. Piers would have heard about John. Embarrassed, she kept walking.

"Hello," Piers called. "Hop on." Buddy was already aboard, sitting with Arthur in the bow. Katie hesitated but since Piers had steered the boat to the side; she had no choice. He stretched his arm to take her hand as she climbed on board.

"I'm glad I saw you this morning. I owe you an apology."

"What? Why?" Katie stammered.

Piers steered into the canal bank and put the engine into neutral. "Bob told me about last night. What a frightening experience. Are you okay? The man in the pub on Saturday; that was John and you weren't there of your own accord."

"Yes. When I left your boat, he was waiting for me outside the cottage. He was uninvited so I wasn't expecting him. I didn't want him in the cottage so I suggested the pub. We are divorced but he's fallen on hard times and wants a reconciliation. I refused and he became aggressive."

"I saw how he pushed you but I overlooked it because I thought you had refused my invite to dine for a boyfriend. I am so very sorry. Can you forgive me?"

"There's nothing to forgive. You couldn't have known."

"I'm curious. Why *did* you leave the boat?"

"Because you had your girlfriend. Not that it matters, except you had never mentioned her and I didn't feel like I belonged." Katie tried hard to sound nonchalant.

Piers laughed and took Katie in his arms. She stiffened as he hugged her.

"Debra?"

"Yes. She was all over you." Katie moved away. Not that she could move far in the cramped space.

"Debra is an old school friend. She devours men but has never found what she is looking for because she doesn't know what she wants. She has been trying to date me since high school. That will never happen. I guess I've become the forbidden fruit. She's also very good at inviting herself, which she did on that occasion, and I don't have the heart to say no. I feel sorry for her; not a sentiment shared by the others. Trust me, I have no romantic interest in Debra."

Piers stared at Katie and her knees almost gave way. His eyes, gentle, kind and tender, seemed to peer beyond the surface. She almost gasped. *What is he seeing?* she wondered.

"Katie, I... I lo... like you very much. I admit, it upset me to see you with John." He took her hand and covered it with both of his, as if to protect her. Already tense, Katie had a fight-or-flight response and pulled away.

Words blurted out of her mouth. She needed to change the subject. "I can't see straight. It's all too much. John's behaviour is troubling." Her throat tightened. The words were irrational.

Piers stepped back, releasing her hand. "Do you still have feelings for him?"

"Oh, heavens no!" Katie coughed, realizing how forceful she sounded.

Piers' head leaned to one side, his expression quizzical.

"Then what is it?"

"His behaviour. He's changed. I know people change over time but this is different. His whole personality has altered. Something is very, very wrong."

"Can you explain what is different?" Piers' tone had switched to practical, even professional. The tenderness that had frightened Katie was gone. She gave a big sigh of relief and paused to gather her thoughts before describing the events. John's midlife crisis, his new love for fast cars and young women resulting in the divorce. How he frittered away all their savings on a fancy condo, ultimately losing everything, including his job. The law associates didn't trust him anymore with clients and then there was his aggressive, abusive behaviour towards Katie. Piers listened, paying attention to every word.

"What about his physical appearance? I don't want to put words in your mouth, but his dress, mannerisms?"

"He's jumpy and agitated. His eyes dart from one thing to another and at other times, his expression is blank. His forehead is often beaded with sweat and the slightest thing angers him. He never used to be like that. John was even tempered, kind and loving. He was outgoing and fun, taking pride in his looks. Now his clothes are dirty and hang off him because he's lost weight."

Piers rubbed his chin and made a few sounds. "I rarely diagnose without seeing the patient but given what you've said, the symptoms indicate addiction. If John were a patient of mine, I would look for symptoms of drug addiction, particularly cocaine. It is prevalent in professional groups because it's expensive. It starts as a recreational drug and quickly becomes addictive."

The blood drained from Katie's face and her head spun like a top. Piers was probably right. The police had suggested the addiction centre, she had thought alcohol, but it made sense now. It was for cocaine addiction.

Piers put his arm around her. "Here, sit down. I'm sorry. That was a shock."

"How can I help him?" she asked.

"I can give you the names of organizations that can help but it will be a struggle to get John to cooperate. He has to want to quit." Piers brushed her cheek, his eyes gentle and understanding, no longer the doctor. "I'm always here for you. Call me anytime." He moved in towards her and, for a second, she thought he might kiss her. A horn blasted from behind, breaking the moment and Katie turned to see another narrowboat approach. Piers waved and put the engine into drive, easing *Tranquil Days* from the canal bank. Steering into the middle, he pointed the bow towards the marina.

After tying the boat to its mooring, he helped Katie out of the boat.

"I have to go. My patients are waiting. I meant what I said, though. Call me anytime."

Katie nodded, waved goodbye, and called Buddy. As she and Buddy walked to the cottage, she realized the relationship with Piers had, perhaps, evolved beyond friendship.

Nineteen

Hope

᪥

A dam and Sir Walter were in the rose garden, deep in conversation, when Katie returned. She slid through the front door, not wanting to talk to anyone and sat down in the guest's lounge. She tried to make sense of what had just happened on the boat. Every time Piers entered her mind, her heart beat faster. He had told her he liked her, and she had not missed the correction from lo…, *Was he going to say love? Don't be ridiculous,* she thought. He's a doctor and knows how to be gentle and empathetic. He's trained to make people trust him. *I'm reacting to his kindness and bedside manner. And he has John pegged.*

Katie felt a sense of relief at Piers' explanation of John. She felt sorry for him though, finding no comfort in being right. John was not himself. She understood little about drug addiction and, unless she had seen it with her own eyes, she would never have believed the destruction it caused. Despite her limited knowledge, she knew that some people never kicked the habit. Would John be one of those? If he was one of the lucky ones, and beat the addiction, could he be his old self again? What were the implications for Katie? She was no longer the mousy housewife. She had aspirations for a better life that did not include an ex-husband. She was content to leave the past in the past, but would John?

The front door opened and jolted Katie from her thoughts. For a brief second, she feared he had returned.

"Mum, what are you doing in here?"

"Oh, Melanie, I am glad to see you. I thought it might be your father."

"Nope, he's in jail. That's what I came to talk to you about. I heard about last night. The police called me to bail Dad out." Melanie gave a sheepish smile. "Forgive me, Mum, but I refused. Phil and I talked about it and decided if he wouldn't go to the treatment centre, then he could sit in jail."

"You did the right thing. Piers gave me his medical opinion. He suspects he's addicted to cocaine." Katie swallowed hard. "And I agree."

Melanie gave a grim smile. "That's what the police said."

Tears moistened Katie's eyes. "What do we do now?"

"Mum, you do nothing. You're divorced. Dad is no longer your responsibility."

"It's not that easy."

"Let me be blunt. Do you love Dad? Would you go back to him?"

"No. I've moved on, but I can't just leave him to cope with this."

"You can't help Dad. He has to do this himself, with professional help."

"Will he consent to treatment?" Katie asked.

"Phil is with him now. He wants to get out of jail. The withdrawal symptoms are starting, prompting him to see a doctor. That was early this morning. Phil will call me when there's news."

"I'll make coffee and we can talk."

"Mum, I have to go. I just popped in on my way to class. Phil took the day off and I'll see him at lunchtime. We'll come by later and let's hope Dad will be in the addiction centre by then." Melanie kissed and hugged her mother. "Try not to worry."

Katie opened the front door and waved goodbye to her daughter. She yawned. Her energy was drained and it wasn't even lunchtime.

Sir Walter wandered through the lounge and attempted to use the Keurig machine. He hadn't seen Katie on the sofa and she smiled at his puzzled expression. "Can I help?" she said.

"I didn't see you there. Yes, please. I can't remember which button to push." He turned and stared at Katie. "You could do with a cup of tea too."

"A cuppa sounds perfect. Why don't I boil the kettle and make a pot?" Sir Walter relaxed. "Come into the morning room and I'll make some proper tea."

Sir Walter carried the tray of tea to the patio and Adam joined them. A normal conversation about the weather and the roses allowed her to let go of the intense emotions that were paralyzing her. She wanted to be clear and objective about John's situation especially after releasing the responsibility to Melanie and Phil. They worked as a couple, comfortable with each other. Their bond and trust was clearly more than just romance.

What was it she was seeing in Piers? She felt affection but

she wondered if she was imagining it. Is Piers responding to her vulnerability?Is he being honest about Debra? And what about the sister-in-law? She knew nothing about him. Was he married? Divorced? In a partnership?

"Penny for them," Adam said.

"Sorry. I'm so tired."

"Go back to bed. Walter and I can manage."

"Lunch needs making and what if guests call for bookings?"

"I can't speak for Adam," Sir Walter said, "but I could do with a pint and Cornish pasty for lunch."

"Gardening is thirsty work. The pub sounds good. Let the answering machine take calls."

Katie hesitated, not wanting to shirk her duties, but the exhaustion was making her feel sick. She needed to rest.

"Mum, are you okay?" Melanie's voice drifted into Katie's dreams. "Mum, wake up. I've brought you tea. Mum!"

Katie opened her eyes to find Melanie on the bed at her side, holding a cup and saucer. "Oh dear, I was sound asleep. What are you doing here? Is everything alright?" She sat up and took the tea. "What time is it?"

"5 o'clock. Adam said you'd been sleeping since noon. Are you ill?"

"No, just tired but the sleep did me good. Is Phil here too?"

"He's downstairs, talking to Adam. We have lots to tell you."

"I'll freshen up. You go on. I'll be down in a minute."

Melanie leaned over and gave her a kiss. "Things will work out, Mum."

Katie put a clean blouse on and brushed her cheeks with blush, adding lipstick before she joined Melanie, Phil and

Adam on the porch. Doris' chair was rocking and Katie was comforted that she was listening in. Doris' ghostly state meant she viewed situations in a different way.

It was one of those pleasant summer evenings, late enough that the bright sunshine had softened and early enough for the evening breeze to be warm. Melanie opened a bottle of cold Pinto Grigio and poured a glass for Katie. Phil stood up and, saying nothing, gave her a hug. Katie felt his reassurance as he spoke. "I have good news about John."

Adam stood up. "Well, I should leave you to it."

"No, Adam, please stay. You're part of the family," Katie added.

"If you're sure." Adam glanced at Melanie and sat down again.

Phil took Melanie's hand and the seat next to her. "The police arrested John last night and he called Melanie to post bail. She refused. We gave John an ultimatum this morning. Either agree to getting treatment or stay in jail. At first, he chose the latter, but as the withdrawal symptoms increased, he began to waiver. I insisted they call a doctor. The police were not cooperative until lunchtime. Out of nowhere, a doctor appeared, one who is a specialist in addiction." Phil took a sip of wine and glanced at Melanie.

"Dad became agitated." Melanie bit her bottom lip. "They waited too long and Dad's paranoia had set in. He insisted the doctor was a spy, out to kill him." She paused. "It's hard to watch as your father's mind retreats into horror. The fear in his eyes was… real. He was terrified." Melanie gulped back a sob and Phil took her hand.

"It's okay, honey. I'll take over." He looked at Katie as a single tear spilled from the corner of her eye. "Perhaps we should take a break?"

Katie brushed her face. "Melanie, do you want to stop?"

"Let's finish." Melanie pulled a tissue from the box. "I'm fine."

"John refused to see the doctor. No amount of talking would persuade him otherwise but suddenly his mood changed. He agreed to talk to the doctor if you, Katie, were in the room. Melanie suggested she would stay. That appeased John and he agreed.

Melanie picked up the tale. "Long story short, this doctor was amazing. He calmed Dad down until he seemed rational. He may have given him something but I couldn't be sure. His questions were so clever that Dad agreed he needed treatment and signed the forms. Because his anxiety was so high, the doctor suggested I go with him in the ambulance. We were at the Darlington Clinic in less than half an hour. Phil followed in the car." Melanie nudged Phil to take over.

"The place is very much 'tough love.' No visitors and compliance to a strict routine of personal, medical and psychiatric care for a month. The patients are not allowed any outside contact. All enquires from us have to go through the proper channels for updates on his progress." Phil turned to Katie and squeezed Melanie's hand. "It will be hard for you two, but necessary, if the treatment is to be successful. The doctor warned us that not all patients complete the program. They have the right to sign themselves out after two weeks. Even if they finish, the success rate is less than 50 percent."

"But it's a start," Melanie interjected. "And the doctor said Dad had a better chance than most of a full recovery. He'd have a clearer picture in about a week."

"Is he alright?"

"Dad's very ill, Mum. As soon as we arrived at the clinic, a male orderly took him in a wheelchair to his room. I didn't talk to him, except in the ambulance. He just kept saying 'I'm sorry, I'm sorry. Tell your mum I'm sorry.'"

Tears prickled Katie's eyes and the same sense of sadness that she had experienced watching John get into the police car, returned. *How had it come to this?*

"Is it a nice place? Will he be looked after?"

"Yes, Mum. The place was clean and it had a warm atmosphere. The staff, although firm, are kind and gentle and Dad will be comfortable."

"I envisioned an old dingy mental hospital, somewhat Dickensian." Katie smiled at her own stereotyping.

"The public mental hospitals are better than Dickens, but this is a private clinic."

"How's he going to pay for it? He couldn't pay his rent last week."

"Dad still has a private medical plan. I took his card from his wallet when we signed him in."

"Didn't he lose that when the firm fired him?"

Melanie shook her head. "Dad wasn't fired. When I spoke to Dad, he said he was on a leave of absence. But without clients, he wasn't getting paid."

"That's why he has the medical insurance. Why would he tell me they'd fired him? Anyway, I'm glad he's in a private clinic." Katie was relieved. She didn't want the responsibility of looking after John. She felt sorry for him, but comfortable, knowing he was being taken care of. There was no doubt in her mind that she no longer loved him. The spark and love she had for John in her twenties had never wavered until a year ago, and now it was dead. She tried hard to remember the love, shocked when similar feelings brought Piers to mind. Guilt consumed her and she looked up to see Melanie staring.

"Mum, what is it?"

Katie nodded and walked inside to the kitchen. "I must start dinner."

"Don't worry about dinner. We'll go to the pub," Melanie said following her in.

Katie leaned on the counter. "I'm overwhelmed. It's hard to reconcile that the man I once loved is in deep trouble and I pity him." She looked at Melanie, tears burning her eyes. "I feel so guilty."

"Oh, Mum, don't. You moved on. There is nothing wrong with that. I'll take care of Dad." She pulled Katie into a hug. "Dad was the one that left you and turned to drugs, all choices he made. None of this is your fault and you have nothing to be guilty about."

"There's more." Katie shifted her eyes to her feet. "I might have feelings for another man." She smiled at Melanie. "That's part of the guilt."

Melanie smiled her approval. "I'm pleased. You deserve a good man. I hope he is a good man."

"I'm not sure. He doesn't talk about himself much and I keep wondering if he has a secret life. We're just friends, no more."

"Are you going to tell me his name?"

"Piers Bannister. He's a doctor and has a boat, *Tranquil Days*. His dog, Arthur, plays with Buddy."

"Piers sounds like a nice man. Starting out as friends works. Phil and I were just friends." Melanie blushed. "We're more than that now, dating, but not living together. Does that sound old fashioned?"

"Old fashioned I like. I see how you are together so I'm not surprised. Are wedding bells in the future?"

"We're talking about it. He's reluctant to propose and I can't figure out why. He says he loves me and I love him very much."

"Marriage is a big step for a longtime bachelor. He's a cautious man and something of a loner. He'll propose when he's ready."

"Maybe you're right."

"Does this mean you won't be going back to Peru?"

"I've considered it but I don't have the same desire as I did before. I loved working on the project and it was a disappointment when they shut it down. But finding Phil has filled a void in my life. We've talked about travelling together, for pleasure. It's unlikely we'd both get sent on an overseas project." She smiled and shrugged her shoulders. "I'm content at the moment."

"It does my heart good to see you happy. Phil is a good man. We just need to get your brother sorted out now."

"Ben's doing fine. I had an email yesterday. Typically brief and to the point. He likes New York and the job is going well. He's worried about Dad, of course. My instinct tells me they'll both be okay."

Katie nodded. "I wish Ben would write more but I'm glad you keep in touch and like you, my sense is that your father will pull through."

Melanie checked her phone. "No messages. That's good. I'm hungry. Shall we eat?"

Twenty

B&B Success

*K*atie sighed, brushing the moisture from her forehead. "I don't ever remember it being this hot in early July and there is no more room at the inn," she said putting the phone down. "That's the third booking I've turned away this morning."

"Did you say something, Ms. Saunders?"

"Oh, Lydia. No, I was talking to myself. We are booked solid throughout July and August and I keep turning people down. I wish I could wave a magic wand and produce two more bedrooms."

"Why don't you build an extension? My dad did that when my mum had the twins." Lydia chuckled and gave an impish grin. "I have my own room, which doesn't go down well with my older brothers and younger sisters as they share."

"How many?"

"Two older brothers and two younger sisters. With the twins, that makes seven of us. Until the twins came along, I shared with my sisters. Dad built on two small bedrooms; a nursery for the twins and, as the eldest girl, I got my own room."

"Hum... An extension. That's not a bad idea but, now, back to work. Can you make up the small room for Sir Walter? He's coming in early today. The double room is for Dr. and Mrs. Larkin. They should arrive late tonight. When you've done that, take a break and get a glass of cold lemonade. I'm making some for the guests. Coffee and tea are too hot today. I'll leave a jug in the fridge. Help yourself." Katie wiped her forehead again, wondering how Lydia could look so cool.

The girl picked up her basket of cleaning materials and Katie watched her bounce up the stairs. She poured herself some lemonade and sat in the shade of the porch, grateful for Lydia's help. One of the best things I ever did was hire Lydia. Just fifteen, Lydia was a breath of fresh air; always happy and cheerful, polite with the guests and a good and willing worker. It was obvious she'd learned from her mother and her housekeeping skills were excellent. Lydia had approached Maisie at the pub for a summer job. Because she was too young to serve alcohol, Maisie has suggested she talk to Katie. A hard worker herself, Maisie had recognized that Katie was barely coping with the fully booked B&B. Katie didn't need to be asked twice and hired Lydia on the spot.

A gentle breeze wafted on to the porch and Katie glanced at the empty chairs. One was rocking to and fro. She had company. Doris' soft whisper floated on the breeze. *'What's troubling you, my dear?'*

The ice clinked in Katie's glass, sounding too loud as she sipped. "Good morning, Doris. I'm not sure, but I sometimes wonder if I did the right thing, opening the B&B. I didn't expect it to be so successful," she added, with a nervous giggle. "That's kind of silly, of course. I want it to be successful. What is bothering me?"

'It's not the B&B, is it?'

"You mean John? Perhaps. He's been at the clinic a long time. Melanie says he's getting better. Doris, I worry he'll get better and I worry he won't. Either way, his life will change." She paused. "I'm afraid it will change mine too."

'I understand about John. You need not worry. He will get better and move on. That's not all, is it? What about Piers?'

"He's just a friend." Katie heard the snap in her voice and her heart pinched.

Doris's chair rocked harder, her words more than a whisper. *'Really! You're in denial, Katie.'*

She sighed. "You're right. I'm afraid my feelings for Piers are more than friendship but I can't be sure of his for me. I wonder if he has a secret past. I'm afraid I'll find out he's married or has a girlfriend or isn't the person I thought he was."

'Piers has a past, a sad one. He will tell you when he's ready. You're expecting he'll hurt you. You're afraid he's not what he seems to be or that he will be unfaithful. Deep in your heart, you realize he isn't married and there are no girlfriends. Could you be using these thoughts to keep him away?'

Katie took a breath to protest, but exhaled instead. "Right again, Doris. I sound as though I'm making excuses but something else is bothering me. Loyalty. When I'm with Piers, I feel as though I'm being disloyal to John. How can I be loyal to both?"

'You can't, my dear. Loyalty to John is in your past. If you can't get over that, you need to question your feelings for him.'

"I'm not sure I have any, beyond sympathy for another

person."

*'There's your answer. I would say, quite bluntly, get over it or it will affect your relationship with Piers.*She went silent as the wind howled through the porch. *'A storm is coming. Tell Adam I'll talk to him later. Did that help?'*

"Yes. Thank you." The wind drove through the porch, knocking over the plant pots and moving the empty chairs. Thunder rumbled in the distance and black clouds appeared overhead.

"At least the storm will bring cooler weather," Adam called out. He hurried in from the garden, just as the rain poured in torrents and an enormous clap of thunder vibrated the porch. "I'm going inside."

Katie sat and watched the storm, enjoying the coolness of the wind and the spray from the rain on her face and limbs. Her thoughts were focused on the conversation with Doris.

Later that evening, Katie left Adam in charge of the B&B. She drove to Autumn Road to join Phil and Melanie for dinner, and to discuss John's progress. One disadvantage of the B&B was a lack of privacy as guests wandered in and out. It wasn't the place to discuss John's demise. Turning the corner onto the old family street gave Katie a sense of trepidation. Her old home looked no different than any of the other houses. The memories of the happy family life with John and the children were no longer associated from the physical place. The experience of being in the old neighbourhood, combined with Doris' earlier advice, had broken the cords to her past. Autumn Road was just another street and John, as he was, just another person. *While living here, I was the mousy housewife, content with my husband and children. Now I'm a self-confident, purpose-driven woman. I don't belong here anymore.*

Her smile spread from cheek to cheek as she knocked on Phil's door.

"Mum, come in," Melanie said, giving her a look and a peck on the cheek. "You look happy."

"I am. I guess you could say I just had an epiphany and came to terms with the past."

Phil's deep voice replied. "You are a strong woman, Katie. It was only a matter of time before you figured it all out. Come into the family room. I'll pour a glass of wine to celebrate." Phil gave her hug and she felt the comfort of his familiarity. He had been her support through some tough times.

Melanie poured the wine and they raised their glasses. "To Katie!"

"Thank you, both of you. Now, how are you two? And why am I here?"

"I need to tend to dinner," Melanie called as she entered the kitchen. "I'm listening, but I'll let Phil bring you up to date on Dad."

"How's he doing?"

"He's doing well. He's over the withdrawal and is managing the cravings. The doctor, nurses and his case worker met yesterday and are ready to discharge him, under supervision." Phil hesitated and glanced at Melanie. "John's coming to stay with us, at least with me, as Melanie isn't here all the time." Phil smiled. "Not yet, anyway." Melanie came to sit on the couch next to Katie and Phil continued. "At first, John will be here on the weekends when we are home and return to the clinic during the week. If that goes okay, he will be allowed to move in with frequent visits to the clinic for therapy. That will be

184

the real test, if he can cope unsupervised when we are at work. As soon as he recovers, and can afford it, he will then be able to move into a place of his own."

"Before we went ahead, we wanted to know how you felt about Dad being here."

"It sounds promising. I'm pleased he's doing so well and it's good that he lives with you at first. I'm fine with that. It might be awkward when I visit, at first, of course. How does your father feel about meeting up with me?"

"He knows it's over. As the drugs left his system, he was able to rationalize. Dad understands you've moved on and he plans to do the same. He's keen to work again and intends to approach the partners when he's well enough." Melanie watched her mother carefully.

"He loved his job," Katie said. "Being involved with work gave him purpose. I hope they take him back. When are you expecting him to arrive?"

"He's coming for the day on Sunday and for the whole weekend next Friday."

Melanie disappeared into the kitchen again and Phil ushered Katie into the dining room. She smiled, calling out. "The table looks lovely. Grandma's dinner service suits your table."

"Thank you," Melanie said, placing a steaming dish of chicken à la king on the table. "I wanted this to be a special occasion and I learned from the best." Melanie bent down and kissed her mother's cheek. "When I was little, I used to creep downstairs and watch you entertain guests. I was convinced you had a private connection with the Palace and learned to set the table like the Queen's. Then I imagined being a princess in a fancy ball gown with a footman escorting me to the table where my prince waited."

"That is so sweet. I never realized. Science was all you talked about. This smells and looks wonderful. You were a good student. What are we celebrating?"

Phil took Melanie's hand, kissed it and they stared at each other. "Phil has proposed and we plan to get married in September. Mum, we wanted to tell you first." She stretched her arm across the table and her left hand sparkled with a sapphire and diamond ring, set in white gold.

"Wow! It's beautiful." Katie grinned with pleasure. "I am pleased and excited for you. Phil, welcome to the family. Although we've known you so long you already feel like family. I never imagined you would be my son-in-law when you moved into the neighbourhood."

Wedding plans topped the conversation for the rest of the evening. To Katie's delight, the wedding would take place in Springsville outside in the rose garden at Lavender Cottage.

The summer passed quickly. Katie hardly had time to breathe with the B&B full of guests every weekend. During August, even the weekdays were booked, mostly with families. The waiting list grew longer and she hated turning people away. She even considered Lydia's idea of building an extension. If there's enough money from the bookings, she could start in the autumn, after the wedding.

Katie had expected the bookings to ease off in September when school started, but a whole new set of guests arrived; retirees who didn't want to fight the high season. Fortunately, she had blocked off the weekend of September 15th for the wedding. The other weekends were booked until the end of October.

She pretended that she didn't mind being shut out of the wedding arrangements, allowing Melanie and Phil to make their plans. But honestly, she was hurt. A Nottingham company even had the privilege of catering. As impractical as it was, she wished Melanie had asked her. She felt left out of all the arrangements, losing her romantic vision of mother and daughter planning every detail of the nuptials. She knew she should discuss her feelings but she didn't want to upset Melanie, aware that she was being considerate because of the B&B. Melanie thought she was doing the right thing in not burdening her mother with wedding plans. The unspoken words resulted in tension.

Twenty-One

Endings and Beginnings

Katie and Buddy walked daily along the towpath. It didn't matter how busy she was; they both needed the fresh air and Katie needed downtime. It was time to think, for her introverted self to re-energize. If Piers was on the boat, he always floated up the canal as Katie and Buddy returned. It amused her that they both pretended to meet by accident when, clearly, the timing was planned. There was no sign of *Tranquil Days* that day. Piers had guests coming from Nottingham. Katie was invited to join them but declined, claiming that she needed to be at the B&B.

Piers' partner Rick Larkin, and wife Cindy, preferred to stay at the B&B rather than on the boat. Katie enjoyed Cindy's company and a friendship was blossoming. Cindy had rolled her eyes, saying that Debra had invited herself, again. She added that Debra was unfair, making Piers give up his bed but was probably hoping to share it. Piers slept on the too small seat in the living area. Katie had accepted Piers explanation of Debra's presence, and Cindy confirmed the sleeping arrangements. Despite the reassurance, a tiny doubt persisted. It was easier to stay away.

It had been weeks since they had talked about Debra. Piers had declared he liked Katie, even hinting the love word, but nothing more had happened. She saw the brief glances, tingled at his touch and felt his heart beat faster when they hugged a greeting. Several times, Piers moved to kiss her but it never happened. As comfortable as they were together, whenever she tried to get closer, Katie felt an invisible barrier.

Buddy ran around the field and Katie sat on the wooden stile with her knees tucked under her chin. Usually she enjoyed solitude, but today she wanted to talk to Judy. Her friend always challenged her, asking pertinent questions about John or Piers. An unexpected flash went off in her head at the realization that she no longer worried about her ex-husband. She was content to let Melanie take care of him. Doris was right, Piers was the problem.

She missed the Saturday morning walks with Judy and Buddy missed playing with Sam and Lily. Judy's latest engineering assignment had taken her to Germany for the summer but she'd promised to be back for the wedding. She really needed the comfort of a chat with her best friend and decided to Skype her at the hotel. Katie picked up the pace and hurried towards home, Buddy running at her heels.

Skype only rang twice before Judy's voice boomed over the internet. "Katie, I'm so glad you called. How are the wedding plans?"

"Fine, I guess. I'm not involved."

"You sound upset."

"Yes and no. I'm hurt that they didn't ask me to cater the wedding. I know it's because they think I'm too busy with the B&B but I hope that's all it is."

"Of course it is! Have you talked to her about it?"

"Sort of. She asked me to make the wedding cake."

"Spit it out! This is more than catering. What's wrong? Is it John? How's he doing?"

"John is fine, Melanie and Phil are looking after him. The clinic discharged him some time ago and he's working part-time, a trial period, I think. I've moved on. Honest."

"It must be Piers."

"As always, you're right. I don't understand him. Nothing more has happened since June. We meet up regularly on the boat and the way he looks at me; it's more than friendship." Katie hesitated. "That woman, Debra, is at the boat this weekend. If he doesn't have feelings for her, why does he invite her onboard?"

"I can't answer that but you have to make a decision. Either confront him or walk away. In my opinion, he's afraid."

"Afraid! Of what? ME!"

"I'm guessing the past has hurt Piers, extremely badly. He can't bring himself to let you into his world. He's probably facing some demons. Either be patient or, as I said, walk away."

Startled at the prospect of losing Piers, Katie felt her stomach clench. And yet, confronting Piers scared her because he might walk away.

"Sorry, that wasn't helpful. But, that's me. I call it as I see it."

"It is helpful. I have to decide and as usual I'm having trouble. I'll wait until after the wedding because he's my escort. He agreed, albeit with reluctance. It's interesting. He said 'I don't usually do weddings, but for Melanie, I'll make an exception.'"

"That is significant, and tells me he's had his heart broken. Katie, I suggest you treat him with kindness, not ultimatums. I hate to run but my group is getting together for lunch and I have to get dressed. We'll talk soon and I'll be home next week."

"I'll be glad when you're back. We can talk more then. See you soon. Bye!" Katie pressed end. Conversations with Judy always challenged her views. She agreed that Piers' behaviour might be fear of getting hurt. It confirmed her suspicion that Piers had secrets, maybe hurtful ones. Looking at it from a different angle made all the difference and she wondered if Cindy knew about his past.

It was serendipity as she heard a tap on the door and Cindy's voice. "Am I interrupting?"

"Come in. I'll make coffee. I need company. Where's Rick?"

"Piers took Rick into town to get supplies and pick up Debra at the bus station."

Katie's mind jumped into gear. It was the perfect opening to quiz Cindy about Debra. "Why does Piers keep inviting her?"

"It's a long story. Piers doesn't invite her. He just doesn't say no when she invites herself."

"Is there something going on between them?"

Cindy burst out laughing. "No, never! Debra is not Piers' type. Although, what is obvious to others is not obvious to Debra." Cindy paused, frowning. "Debra's always been flighty. We were in grammar school together."

"Piers mentioned that she has been trying to date him for a long time but I didn't realize you all went back that far." Katie tried to sound nonchalant.

"Debra, Piers, Julianne and I hung around together. I didn't meet Rick until college. Julianne was my best friend. She and

Piers were sweethearts. I don't think either of them looked at another person." Cindy hesitated. "He hasn't told you, has he?"

"Told me what?"

"About his wife, Julianne."

"The name was never mentioned." Katie felt her heart plummet to her feet. *Married. Why hadn't he told her?* She felt betrayed. *The looks, the touch, the kindness was it all a farce? I'll sort you out, Piers Bannister. I want to meet this wife. Someone needs to tell her about his roving eye. John did it and I will not be part of infidelity.*

"Katie, what is it?"

"I wasn't aware he was married. He made…advances…but only small ones. I would not have encouraged it, had I known. My ex had affairs and it brings heartache. How come I haven't met Julianne?" Katie handed Cindy a cup of coffee and stared at the sadness and tears in Cindy's eyes. "What am I missing?"

"Julianne died four years ago, after a long battle with cancer. Piers fell apart. He didn't want to live without Julianne. That's when he bought the boat. It gave him peace, floating along the quiet canals. It was, perhaps, his salvation. Debra is a nurse at the palliative care centre and she helped care for Julianne until the end. Piers' gratitude is eternal for the care Debra gave his wife. That's why he never says no." Cindy brushed tears from her cheeks. "I miss her, so much. We were inseparable. She didn't deserve to die so young."

"I am so sorry." Katie felt her cheeks redden with shame for misjudging Piers. She remembered Judy's suggestion that he was afraid. She was right. How would she cope, losing her best friend? Judy was her confidante, her supporter.

"Julianne was an award-winning journalist and foreign correspondent. She covered riots, uprisings and even survived

Afghanistan, only to come home with a diagnosis of terminal cancer."

"I wish Piers had told me."

"He wouldn't say anything. He's too lost without Julianne. He buried himself in work at the clinic until he had a nervous breakdown about a year ago. His recovery has been slow. Having friends at the boat was a big step and inviting you on board shocked me—in a good way. I never thought I'd see the day he'd even glance at another woman."

"We're friends, nothing more. What you just told me confirms that."

Cindy raised her eyebrow. "Really? The way he looks at you reminds me of how he looked at Julianne. He's in love with you and I think it's marvelous. He deserves another chance and so do you."

Katie shook her head. "I don't think so. His heart has been broken into a million pieces and so has mine. We both have trust issues. We have a lot in common as friends and that's okay. Thanks for confiding in me because it's a relief. Now I can be a good friend without any pressure."

"Suit yourself." Cindy's shoulders shrugged as she put the coffee cup in the sink. "I'm heading to Cyril's place. I'm looking for an antique oak gate-legged table for the hall. Do you want to join me?"

"I'm tempted but with a full house I must get back to work."

"I'll see you at dinner then."

"I told Piers I can't make it to dinner."

"Why not? Piers wants you to come. It hurt him the last time you turned down the invite."

"Okay. Tell Piers I changed my mind. I'll see you tonight." Still skeptical about going to dinner, Katie hoped she was doing the right thing. Based on Cindy's account of Debra and the tragic death of Piers' wife, she had a whole new perspective on the situation. It also ruled out any kind of romance.

Katie heard Cindy close the front door and turned to the counter to prepare the fruit for breakfast as voices wafted into the kitchen. Cindy was talking to Phil. Was something wrong? Where was Melanie?

"Hello, Mum," Melanie called from the patio as she entered the French doors. "Surprise!"

"And a lovely surprise it is too. I wasn't expecting you today. Is everything alright?"

"We just dropped Dad off at the centre for a therapy session and decided to pop by."

"How's he doing?"

"Actually, Mum, he's doing much better than expected. The centre is pleased with his progress. The partners have increased his hours but they won't let him work alone and his work is scrutinized, which he finds difficult but it's necessary. The firm is," Melanie paused, "cautiously optimistic. That's lawyer talk for pleased with the progress."

"That is good news. And the wedding plans?"

"Pretty much organized but we'd like your help to choose the menu. Mum, I know you would like to do the catering, but be realistic. It's too much for you with the B&B. But your input would be welcome. We also need to talk about Dad and his part in the wedding."

"We want you to be part of these decisions," Phil said, appearing from the guests' lounge.

"Let's talk about Dad first." The rapid heartbeat surprised Katie. She was nervous about John being at the wedding.

"Mum, I want Dad to give me away. I've talked to Judy and

she suggested she should be his, for want of a better word, date for the wedding."

"That's a great idea. Judy would make sure your dad behaved." Katie blushed. "I've invited Piers, as a friend." Katie was surprised Melanie didn't react.

"What do you think of champagne and finger food? That eliminates any seating plan and suits our idea of a casual reception."

"Without the sit-down meal, everyone can mingle, and it solves a lot of potential problems. The wedding and reception are still here?"

"If it's okay with you. I'd like the ceremony in the rose garden. Do you think Adam would be okay putting up a canopy, just in case of rain? The guest list is less than 40 people. What do you say?" Melanie beamed, waiting for Katie's response.

"Adam will be thrilled to have the rose garden put to good use. If it's raining, we can use the guest lounge and the morning room. Ben sent a message this morning. He plans to arrive on the 13th.

"Phil asked Ben to be best-man." Melanie hesitated. "Phil hasn't any family to invite. His parents died when he was young and he's lost touch with his brother. Poor kids were sent to separate foster homes. Phil has nothing good to say about his foster parents but he'd like to find his brother. As that's not possible for the wedding, Ben is a good substitute."

"I always suspected there was sadness in Phil's past. He never mentioned foster homes or a lost brother but it does explain a few things. I'm looking forward to seeing Ben. It seems ages since he went to America. Have you decided on a colour theme?"

"Champagne pink and pastel green. I have to have green

in my wedding. The caterer talked me out of bright green and suggested a soft, pale spring green. I like it." Melanie dug into her bag and pulled out the menu. "Here are the food suggestions, Mum. What do you think?"

Katie nodded approval. Melanie had chosen well. The simple theme and perfect colours gave Katie the idea of interlaced leaves on champagne pink icing for the wedding cake.

"We made a lot of decisions today but you haven't mentioned a dress."

"I'm not sure what I want. I hate frills and yet a suit style is too plain. Can we go to Nottingham on Monday? I don't have classes."

"Monday it is. I'll meet you downtown, outside Debenhams, at noon."

Nottingham turned out to be a fun mother and daughter day. The perfect dress was purchased and they found a florist who understood Melanie's wish for greenery in a simple bouquet. A quick visit to the caterer confirmed the menu. They ended with a long pleasant dinner, discussing guests, accommodations, gifts and the little things often overlooked.

The wedding had stirred conflicting thoughts in Katie. As mother of the bride, she felt proud of her daughter and soon to be son-in-Law. But it also took her back to her own wedding. She and John had been so in love, so happy. It was one of the happiest days of her life and, in spite of everything, it still was—life had just moved on. And Piers, how would he feel? Reminders of a life and wife he loved very much with an unseen and tragic outcome would be everywhere. There were days Katie wanted the wedding to be over and days she wanted to wrap herself, and all those she loved, in romance and happiness; the happy-ever-after kind. She wondered if she was being unrealistic. Life rarely gave everyone all they wanted, but it did give what was needed. If part of that was happiness, they should embrace what they had and strive for the rest.

A muffled, excited chatter emanated from under the white canopy that protected guests from the anticipated rain. Phil and Ben stood under the arbour, making small talk with the vicar. Katie and John were little more than an arm's length apart in the morning room, waiting for Melanie. Katie smiled at John. "I'm pleased you are able do this for our daughter. Thank you."

"I owe her my life. I owe you all my life. If it wasn't for the support, I wouldn't be here today. It means a lot to me that we can stand together and watch our daughter marry the love of her life." John stepped forward and kissed Katie on the cheek. "You will always be in my heart, Katie. I accept things are different and I'm okay with that."

Melanie walked in. The simplicity of her dress was stunning. A soft scoop neckline and short sleeves in pink champagne silk fitted into her waist and floated to the floor. The bouquet of roses blended with the dress, the soft green foliage a pleasant contrast. A single rose held one side of her hair up and the other side curled onto her shoulder. Her maid of honour, stood behind her in a simple silk dress of the palest green.

"It's time." Katie kissed her daughter, walked through the French doors and down the aisle to take her seat; the signal for the trio to play the wedding march. John looped his arm in Melanie's and escorted her down the aisle. He never took his eyes off his daughter until he handed her to Phil.

Katie's determination not to cry held off until she felt Piers' arm on her waist and the tears trickled down her cheeks. He cupped her chin, took a white linen hanky and brushed the tears away. "She's a beautiful bride. As beautiful as her mother. They will be happy."

"Thanks. Are you all right?"

"Yes. It reminded me of how happy Julianne and I were on our wedding day and I'm grateful for those years we had together. She will always be in my heart but it's time to move on. Julianne never wanted me to grieve away all these years. And you?"

"Sort of the same. We were in love the day we married and I, too, am grateful for the many years of happiness we had together. It's strange, but just before the service John said something similar. 'You'll always be in my heart, Katie.' He gave me permission to move on."

Piers leaned forward and Katie waited, her eyes closed. She held her breath until Piers' warm lips touched hers, gasping as a warm sensation trickled along her spine. She kissed harder, entwining her fingers behind his neck and pulling him closer. Piers' arms tightened around her waist and her feet lifted off the ground. She floated in loving bliss. The kiss lingered on and time stood still, making up for all those times they never kissed. Love had found a way to repair two broken hearts.

The End

My Thanks

Thank you for reading *When Love Ends, Romance Begins- Book 1 of The Narrowboat Romance Series.* If you enjoyed this book, you might enjoy Susan's Readers Group. Join and receive a gift of the e-book of *Ruins in Silk - Prequel to The Sackville Hotel Trilogy* https://dl.bookfunnel.com/hj6embawkt

What Happens Next

Melanie and Phil enjoy a brief weekend honeymoon before settling down to suburban life on Autumn Road. Not a typical suburban family, but a career-orientated couple with goals to reach. Katie will have to wait a while before grandchildren. John stays with his daughter and son-in-law until he can return to practicing full-time, fully recovered.

Prompted by Melanie and the love of his new family, Phil begins to search for his long-lost brother.

Ben found his calling. The jazz band he manages reached international fame because of his marketing skills. He returned to New York, secure in the knowledge that, at last, he had made his father proud.

Lavender Cottage B&B continues to be a great success and the refurbishing expanded the number of guest rooms. Katie settled in as a prominent member of the village community and Adam stayed on as a permanent resident handyman/gardener. He talks to Doris every day and she watches over him and listens to Katie's troubles.

Although Katie and Piers declared their love at Melanie's wedding, obvious to all of Springsville, the village waits for wedding bells. Lost loves and troubled pasts don't easily erase and, at times, haunt Piers and Katie's relationship.

Book 2 & 3 (works in progress) of The Narrowboat Romance Series will bring you more love from the narrowboats of Springsville. Melanie and Phil's wedding is the first of many. Will Piers and Katie resolve their troubles and make Katie one of the Lavender Cottage brides?
Look out for Christmas at Lavender Cottage December 2018

Acknowledgements

Most authors write their books on an island in isolation and I am no exception. But a book is far more than just writing the story; it includes research, consultations and expertise in editing, cover design and formatting.

I would like to thank Meghan Negrijn for working her editing magic on this manuscript and to Nancy Morris for proofreading and catching those pesky typos. Our apologies if we missed any and a note to say, depending where you live in the world, some spelling may be slightly different. Much appreciations goes to my daughter Rosemary Bann for her Adobe expertise needed for the cover.

Thank you to my wonderful friends at TOSS (The Ottawa Story Spinners) Audrey Starkes, Anne Raina, Tony Myres and Rita Myres and to the Historical Writing Ladies, Meghan Negrijn, Susan Taylor Meehan and Margaret Southall for your encouraging words and helpful critiques. I am so grateful for your input.

Also a special mention to my mum, Betty Jennings for her encouragement and for introducing me to Mercia Marina near

Acknowledgements

Willington in South Derbyshire U.K..

Mercia Marina deserves credit for inspiring these stories. It is a beautiful place and well worth the visit. Willow Tree café serves amazing homemade food. Buyers beware—the desserts are amazing. Stillwater Convenience Store displays a selection of delightful gifts, my favourite being the leather narrowboat bookmarks. I believe Mercia Marina is now the largest marina of its kind in Great Britain.

For more information on British narrowboats and Mercia Marina please click on the links below.
Mercia Marina - http://www.merciamarina.co.uk
Wikipedia
https://en.wikipedia.org/wiki/History_of_the_British_canal_system
History of Narrowboats
https://www.waterways.org.uk/blog/evolution_the_narrow_boat

Front cover images:
Couple vector image by Imal8688/Shutterstock
Narrowboat by Kev Gregory/Shutterstock

About the Author

Susan A. Jennings was born in Britain of a Canadian mother and British father. Both her Canadian and British heritages are often featured in her stories. She lives and writes in Ottawa, Canada and is the author of *The Sackville Hotel Trilogy*, which combines historical fiction, a family saga and intriguing love story. Her latest work The Narrowboat Romance Series is quite different, a contemporary romance with an unusual backdrop of an English narrowboat marina. Susan is currently working on another historical series, early 20th century, Sophie, a character you may recognize from the trilogy.

Susan writes a weekly blog *For the Love of Story* and welcomes new subscribers http://susanajennings.com she loves connecting with readers. She is available to speak at book clubs or other events.

Have you ever thought about writing a book? Susan facilitates a variety of writing workshops designed for novice and want-to-be writers. Contact Susan for the schedule. Don't have time for physical attendance? I understand. *First*

Sentence to First Sale a three part, writing course is available online, work at your own pace and on your own time. https://just-for-writers.teachable.com

Contact Susan:

> *Website and Blog: http://susanajennings.com*
> *Facebook author page:*
> *http://facebook.com/authorsusanajennings*
> *Facebook writers page:*
> *http://facebook.com/justforwriterslikeyou*
> *Twitter: http://twitter.com/sajauthor*
> *YouTube :http://youtube.com/SusanAJennings*

More Books

The Sackville Hotel Trilogy
Anna's lifestory from the Edwardian era to the Cold War
of the 60's. Undeterred by stuffy protocol, adventurous
Anna defies Edwardian society and stays ahead of her
time as she takes ownership of the Sackville Hotel and
brings it into the modern age. A story of dreams, romance,
determination, betrayal and love. Whose dream will
ultimately survive; Anna's or granddaughter Sarah's?

Purchase these books from your retailer of choice

The Blue Pendant Book 1
https://books2read.com/u/mlK7YP

Anna's Legacy Book 2
https://books2read.com/u/m2XAxO

Sarah's Choice Book 3
https://books2read.com/u/mlK7YP

Prequel: Ruins in Silk
https://books2read.com/u/bw8DjY

OR
Get you a free e-book gift
of Ruins in Silk e-book
https://dl.bookfunnel.com/hj6embawkt

Join Susan's Readers Groupfor news, discussions and updates
*http://eepurl.com/bgY6kb_*

Writing course
New - *First Sentence to First Sale*
A three-part course for novice and want-to-be writers
Have you every thought of writing a book but don't know where to start?
http://just-for-writers.teachable.com

Printed by Gauvin Press
Gatineau, Québec